Also by Ellis Blackwood

"Among the finest historical cozy mysteries of our time" – Cozy Crime Reads

The Samuel Pepys Mysteries
Mr Pepys's Stolen Diaries (ellisblackwood.com)
Book 1: The Brampton Witch Murders
Book 2: The Plague Doctor Murders
Book 3: The Coffee House Murders
Book 4: The King's Court Murders
Book 5: The Frost Fair Murders
Book 6: The Drury Lane Murders
Book 7: The Brampton Ghost Murders
Book 8: The Crown Jewels Murders
Book 9: Jacob's Last Standish

The Quill & Page Victorian Mysteries

The Brampton Ghost Murders

The Samuel Pepys Mysteries Book 7

Ellis Blackwood

Vintage Mystery Press

Paperback ISBN: 978-1-0687027-9-2

Cover design, editorial & historical fact-checking: Tim Brown, A.S.C. (Rtd).

Ghost cover image licensed from slowbuzzstudio on stock.adobe.com.

For Steve Goldsmith, newsletter competition winner and esteemed Pepysaholic.

*And there went about our great work to dig up
my gold. But, Lord! what a tosse I was for some
time in, that they could not justly tell where it
was; that I begun heartily to sweat, and be angry,
that they should not agree better upon the place.*

From the diary of Samuel Pepys

Scan for website and social media links

Contents

Chapter One

A Troubled Morning

Samuel Pepys lay in bed, eyes darting side to side, hardly daring to breathe. Beside him, his wife, Elizabeth, murmured in her sleep.

Why would she not wake? Had she not heard it?

Knocking.

As if somebody were trying to break a window.

And worse: *footsteps.*

On his stairs.

Thieves? he wondered, throat so very dry. *Or a vengeful spirit?*

Is this house haunted?

It was not the first time the thought had occurred to him. The house on Seething Lane was old, and uncomfortably close to the Tower, where so many had met their untimely end.

Mind racing with visions of his own grisly demise, he nudged Elizabeth until she woke, bleary-eyed and befuddled.

"Hark!" he hissed.

Together, they listened to the sounds, discussing in urgent whispers who - or what - might be causing such disturbance in the early hours.

"What if out servants have been murdered in their beds?" he whispered, pulling the woollen winter blanket tighter around him.

As master of the house, should he investigate?

The prospect filled him with dread, and he was relieved when Elizabeth forbade him from doing so. He had had to offer twice before she obliged.

A good while passed before Pepys dared to rise, grimacing at every creak of the bed for fear of alerting the intruder, corporeal or otherwise. Tugging on his nightgown and breeches, he selected a brass firebrand from the hearth and gripped it tightly.

It felt insufficient.

With a glance at Elizabeth - perhaps his last, it occurred to him - he opened the door and peered into the stairway. Up, then down. His heartbeat pulsed in his ears, and he noticed his hand was trembling.

From downstairs in the pantry he heard movement, and softly called out, "Mary? Mary Blythe?"

The kitchen maid's head appeared through the doorway, hair tied beneath a linen coif, just as a small, dark shape bolted past him on the stairs. He threw himself backwards, emitting a strangled shriek.

The cat. *The confounded cat.*

Later, he would discover that his neighbour was having his chimneys swept, accounting for the other loud noises he had heard. How witless he had been to imagine spectres at work – but then such unquiet apparitions were fresh in his mind.

Pepys resolved to recount none of it to his inquisitors, Abigail Harcourt and Jacob Standish, when they arrived shortly before St Olave's bell chimed the ninth hour across Seething Lane. Abigail first, then a few minutes later, Jacob, each dressed against the city's chill.

It was January 14th, 1667, a Tuesday, and the year thus far had delivered mixed blessings. Abby and Jacob – more she than he, in fairness – had solved the Drury Lane murders, once again drawing the King's notice to their talents, which could only reflect favourably upon Pepys himself.

Yet his household accounts lay in disarray. Several bags of gold coins he had entrusted to his father, to be buried in the garden at Brampton the previous year, had lately been declared missing, most likely stolen.

Their value was considerable. The broad pieces, dating back to Cromwell's Commonwealth, each worth twenty shillings, totalled more than two thousand pounds. His annual salary was 350 pounds - an enviable sum in itself.

It churned his insides to dwell upon it, and more than once he had cried out in anguish.

The things he held dearest to his heart were his work, his wealth and his wife (not necessarily in that order), and one of those had suffered a grievous assault. It was why he had engaged his inquisitors.

The three sat in Pepys's study, its dark-wood walls lined with rows of leather-bound tomes and framed paintings of proud galleons under sail, a reminder of his work as Clerk of the Acts to the Charles II's Navy Board. Expensive candles lit the room, giving off a homely scent of beeswax, while flames from a freshly laid fire licked the sooted walls of the hearth.

Outside, a whistling wind vented its fury, and the leaded windows rattled.

Pepys shuddered.

"Your missing gold, sir?" Jacob said.

Two days ago, when the investigation at the King's Playhouse had been concluded, Pepys had first told his inquisitors of the gaping hole in his accounts. The details he passed on were sparse, since they had been celebrating, and he had been loath to expand upon his foolishness.

How could he, a man of intellect, entrust such a vast sum to another - even his father? John Pepys, once a tailor, now retired to the Brampton countryside in Huntingdonshire, was old, his mind fogged and ailing. That his younger, sole surviving sister, Paulina, had been charged with helping him to bury the hoard caused Pepys more concern than good.

She was a flighty sort, given to outbursts and incorrigible behaviour, with a disturbing taste in suitors. There had been talk of a new man, one Harry Packer, about whom Pepys knew precious little, and it worried him no end.

Who was this Packer fellow? What work did he do - if any - and what dread tales followed his name?

Pepys had visited Brampton himself only a week ago, in a final effort to find his gold, but had left empty-handed and more disconsolate than ever.

Abby fidgeted in her seat. "Mr Pepys?"

He shook himself. "Indeed, Abigail, indeed. I must calm my troubled mind. If only…"

He trailed off.

Jacob glanced across at Abby. She wore a slate-blue woollen coat he had not seen before, its cuffs trimmed with black braid. Now she had removed it, he noticed her burgundy bodice looked new also, and at her throat was an oval brooch of smooth agate set into brass.

Though hardly ostentatious, these were items he knew she could ill afford, even with her new inquisitor's wages.

Were they gifts? he wondered, a sinking sensation settling in his stomach.

Is there a new man in her life? Has she fallen for one of those awful, preening actors she encountered at the theatre?

Then he realised Pepys was speaking.

"…and I toiled all night under the moon's scant light, for fear of being seen. I dug hole after hole, guided by my gibbering father, who made less sense with each utterance. Needless to say, I found nought and could but tear at my hair with filth-encrusted hands."

"Who in Brampton knew of the gold?" Abby asked.

Pepys all but banged his forehead into his desk in frustration. "As far as I can ascertain, all of Brampton knows of the gold!" he wailed. "And may even have done so since the day it arrived there. My father buried it, he admitted to me, one Lord's day after church - in broad daylight! How could anybody…?" A guttural sound emerged from his throat.

It was too much for the poor man to bear.

"Has any of the gold been recovered, sir?" Jacob asked.

Pepys sighed expansively. "Three poxy coins, Mr Standish. Three poxy coins. Found lying on the lawn."

Abby sucked in her lower lip. "Which suggests…"

Pepys sighed again. "Aye, Abigail, which suggests the coins have been unearthed."

"When were the three coins found?" she asked.

"Some while ago now. I assumed – dearly hoped – they had been dropped when the sacks were first buried, yet as time wore on, my concerns only grew. Since my last visit, I can but fear the worst. That my gold is stolen."

Jacob raised a finger. "Two days ago, you told us of…"

"Aye," Pepys cut in. "I told you of a ghost."

Chapter Two

The Drummer

When Pepys first uttered the name "the Wychwood Drummer", Abby heard Jacob gulp and looked across to see his gaunt cheeks blanching. He was a resolute soul who wore his heart on his sleeve, but he had not read the books she had, and was apt to credit all manner of superstition until firmly dissuaded.

The Wychwood Drummer, Pepys explained, was said to be the ghost of one William Rudd, an industrious young lad who had served the Ravenscourt estate in Brampton. Having joined the New Model Army under Cromwell, he returned to his lodgings there once the Protectorate fell, and was accused of stealing a drum from His Lordship. Rudd was hanged for the crime, though the drum was later found in a storeroom at the manor house.

"'Tis said he now haunts the woodland stretching south-east of the estate, toward the Ouse," Pepys concluded. "Woodland known as Wychwood."

"Was there a witch?" Jacob asked, attempting to sound nonchalant. "In the forest?"

Pepys's withering stare told him there was not.

Local tales had the Drummer appearing in Brampton village itself, hovering over the roof of The Bull inn, tapping out a march while imps danced in circles around him. Other times, the beat of his lonely tattoo had been heard drifting across the fields from among the dense woodland – a signal, it was said, for all manner of unholy beasts to wander the land in search of succour.

Farm animals had been found dead in the aftermath, teeth hideously bared, mortal terror trapped in their unseeing eyes.

"And this Wychwood Drummer has been heard again of late?" Abby asked.

Pepys called downstairs for ale. "Aye, 'tis most convenient, do you not think? According to my father, this ghostly apparition now guards my gold, having taken it himself to avenge his execution for thievery.

"That somebody would concoct such a far-fetched tale only confirms for me that my gold has been purloined, by some... by some..." He faltered, unable to find the words, then slammed a fist onto his desk. "And I demand its return!"

Jacob spoke up. "If this ghost of Rudd, as you say, guards the gold. Then..." He stopped.

Pepys's brown eyes bulged. "Aye, spit it out, Jacob."

"Then to find the gold, we must first find," the inquisitor grimaced, "the ghost."

Pepys and Abby were compelled to remind him of their previous investigation in Brampton, when Pepys's sister, Paulina, and her friend, Rebecca Thacker, had been accused of witchcraft.

"Falsely accused, Jacob," Abby pointed out. "Those poor women were no more witches than you or I."

He managed a pale smile. "Then witch-finders…"

"Are charlatans, Mr Standish," said Pepys. "Godless men claiming piety who terrorise rural communities for bounty. If I had my way, they would all be hanged."

Abby's turquoise eyes flashed. "Should ghosts exist…"

"Should ghosts exist," Pepys cut in, "I shall eat my periwig!"

Mary Blythe appeared at the door. "Your ale, sir. I hope I'm not…"

"Nay, you are not. Enter, enter, and hurry, would you?" Pepys gestured impatiently. "My throat is parched from all this vexing discourse."

As she poured, Mary cast a teasing look at Abby's new brooch.

The inquisitor smiled at her friend, stroking the agate. "A gift," she said quietly.

Jacob felt his neck stiffen.

"…to myself," Abby added.

The ale had been warmed and spiced to help stave off the cold, and its mingling aromas of nutmeg, clove and cinnamon drew a veil of calm over the room.

Abby asked how the gold had been taken to Brampton from Seething Lane. "Did you ride with it yourself?"

Pepys picked a clove from his teeth. "I dearly wish I had."

He had arranged transport of the sacks of gold via the Navy Office, whose messengers he believed he could firmly trust. "And indeed, they arrived safely and in good order, which my father confirmed to me." He hesitated.

"Yet…?" Abby pressed.

"Yet I have since been unable to discover the identity of the messenger who rode with it. One clerk points me to another, and none take responsibility for the appointment." Pepys sighed. "Such is the way of the King's offices."

"Then this messenger could have been the one to spread word of your hoard?"

Pepys nodded dolefully, and the three sat in silence for a while.

At length, Jacob spoke. "You have not told us why you sent your gold away, sir."

It happened early the previous year, Pepys explained. The Dutch War was raging, and word had reached him that the Dutch fleet meant brazenly to sail up the Thames into London. "Had they succeeded, they would have looted our homes. 'Twas a chance I dared not take. I…"

"How many sacks of gold were there?" Abby asked.

Pepys groaned. "Five, Abigail. Five." He spoke as if he could not believe it himself. "And heavy with it."

St Olave's bell chimed the tenth hour.

"When do we leave for Brampton, sir?" Jacob asked.

Buoyed by his inquisitor's eagerness, Pepys rose and puffed out his chest. "Why, now, Mr Standish. This very instant. Time is precious. With each passing hour, some despicable miscreant might be spending my hard-won coin."

Chapter Three

Discord

Abby and Jacob's route by hackney coach, following London Wall from Aldgate to Cripplegate, returned ill memories. The last time they had undertaken the journey, it had been on the morning the devastating fire took hold of the city.

From the high vantage point, as London sloped down toward the Thames, and with so many buildings already levelled, the extent of the destruction - and the flames' unquenched hunger - was all too apparent. Each remembered their sense of helplessness, the overwhelming sorrow, and yet the relief that they were leaving it all behind.

Abigail and Jacob had been mere strangers then, having met only that evening, placed together by fate, fortune and Samuel Pepys. One moment, Abby was scrubbing out Pepys's chamber pot; the next, she was being whisked into the Huntingdonshire countryside to save his sister from a witch-finder's clutches.

It had all happened so fast, it felt like a fevered dream.

She recalled her first sight of Jacob Standish, the unusually tall man with bushy eyebrows that met as one, his stretched, bony face and his earnest, almost boyish expression. He was twenty-two years old, yet could have passed for younger.

Ungainly and dishevelled, prone to toying with his tatty periwig in times of discomfort, he had seemed hopelessly out of his depth.

For Jacob's part, he remembered their introduction all too clearly. How his impression of Abby had changed since that day.

She was a handsome young woman, petite yet hardly feeble, with flame-red hair that trailed in wisps down her freckled cheeks, and a pout that spoke of insolence. The manner in which she had spoken to Mr Pepys that first night… He would have had her thrashed.

Yet how wrong he was. While her audacious manner might still cause him to wince, he now felt he understood her. She had fought her way up from Southwark's poverty, had been taught to read and write by her printer father, then taken under Pepys's wing, doggedly seizing every opportunity to advance herself.

So few in her situation would have mustered such temerity. There was something about Abigail Harcourt – unlike any other woman Jacob had met; unlike most men, in truth. She had the keen mind and grim determination to force her way in the world. It had irritated, even offended him, at first, yet he had grown to admire her for it.

With admiration, over time, had come a form of affection.

They had saved each other's lives – at the King's court and on the bank of the frozen Thames (the less said about the theatre, the better) – which could only bring them closer together. For sure, he loved her as a brother loves a sister. More so even than his own sisters.

But is it more than that?

If only he could decide.

They were seated beside each other, facing Pepys, in the stagecoach bound for Huntingdon. From experience, they knew it would stop first at Stevenage, where they would rest overnight at the King's Arms.

As the coach lurched, Pepys adjusted his heavy velvet coat and beige waistcoat, his periwig sitting perfectly in place beneath a plumed, wide-brimmed hat. Abigail pulled her coat tight about her bodice – finer quality than her old servant's garb, her dark skirts remaining practical.

Jacob wore his usual attire: black coat, rumpled shirt and baggy breeches, his long limbs fighting for space in the cramped interior. He, too, wore a periwig and hat, yet his looked as if it had been wrested from a vagrant.

The dirt road was frozen, making the going trouble-some. The shutters were closed against a burgeoning gale, the wooden cab in near darkness, and all were grateful not to be seated up front with the coachman.

"You bought yourself a brooch?" Jacob asked her, hoping it sounded offhand.

"I did wonder the same," Pepys added, righting himself as they were thrown to one side when the coach wheels hit a rut.

Grinning, Abby opened her coat, unclasped the brooch and handed it to Pepys. He held it close to their single lantern for inspection, grunted approval, and passed it to Jacob - who returned it to Abby without a glance.

She gazed at her fellow inquisitor, squinting. "Don't you like it? 'Tis agate. My favourite colour."

Jacob cleared his throat. "I am well aware of the stone. And you purchased it yourself?"

"Alongside that coat and bodice, I'll wager," said Pepys, then in an oily voice added, "Is there… an admirer? At the King's Playhouse, perhaps? Mr Lucius seemed most taken with you, the incorrigible rogue."

"I…" Abby began, but Jacob leapt in.

"Dorian Lucius is a lecherous cur who would," he spluttered, "…who would lay with a sow if it allowed him."

Abby allowed the resulting silence to linger awhile. "I was rewarded for my work at the theatre by Mr Tresillion, the manager, who gave me the coat and bodice. Why," she paused, soaking up the attention, "he even offered me a permanent place in the King's Company."

Pepys sat back, flabbergasted. Jacob's eyelid twitched.

Just then, the coach wheels struck a particularly deep rut. Pepys and Abby braced themselves as Jacob toppled stiffly forward, ending in a heap at his employer's feet.

Wordlessly, he picked himself up, dusted himself down and retook his seat. Aware of his clumsiness, the others acted as if nothing had happened.

"You did not accept Mr Tresillion's generous offer?" Pepys asked.

Abby gestured around her. "Would I be here if I had?"

She had meant it in jest.

Jacob glared daggers, while Pepys drew a sharp breath.

She smiled weakly. "Forgive me, sir, I beg you. I spoke out of turn."

Pepys's eyes narrowed. "Indeed you did. Were it not for me, you would be back scrubbing floors like any common serving wench."

"The King's stage is not for you, Abigail, and such airs ill become you," Jacob added haughtily. "Remember your place." The moment the words left his mouth, he regretted them.

Though stung, Abby kept her counsel. How quickly the men had turned.

Is that what they truly believe?

Taking to the stage at the King's Playhouse had been the toughest test of her life, harder even than learning the trade of inquisitor. And she had passed with flying colours, judging by the audience's applause.

How those Londoners had cheered and hollered their appreciation. The cries of "Bravo!" still rang in her ears. The other actors had accepted her as one of their own, despite her rawness. She had never even seen a play performed before, yet had triumphed upon the King's stage while rooting out a murderer in its tiring house.

She remembered too well the days when her belief in herself was sorely lacking, even as she fought against it.

Those days, she thought, *must be banished.*

The remainder of the journey to Stevenage passed without discourse.

Chapter Four

Supper

Their backsides numbed and their bones shaken, the travellers gratefully stepped off the coach footplate onto the hay-strewn ground of the King's Arms' courtyard. The four sturdy horses up front shook their heads, steaming from their exertions, having galloped near thirty miles without rest from Cripplegate.

A servant appeared and bade them enter the inn, then joined the coachman to unload their luggage. The inquisitors gazed up and around. Stabled horses regarded them curiously, and overhead the stars shone with an abundance only the countryside could offer.

Jacob caught Abby's eye and smiled.

She returned the gesture.

The unpleasantness of the journey seemed already forgotten.

Having retired to their separate guest rooms to wash and change, Pepys, Abby and Jacob reunited in the inn's tap-room. The thick, lined oak beams sat low over-head, and a joint of beef turned slowly on a spit before the fire. Jacob licked his lips in anticipation.

A long wooden counter sat to one side, behind which the innkeeper and his boy worked the taps, drawing cloudy brown ale from barrels stacked against the wall. At trestle tables set about the room, trav-ellers, drovers and townsfolk sat shoulder to shoulder, tankards in hand, imbibing with good cheer.

Pepys ordered a platter of beef with carrots, parsnip, turnip and pease pudding, as well as pigeon pie and a loaf of maslin bread. He professed himself ravenous, blaming the country air and lack of dinner.

Nor was he alone. Though the food set before them all but covered the table, it was gone in a trice, as if spirited away.

Jacob, loosening his belt, let out a contented belch.

"I've been thinking, sir," said Abby, "about the three coins found in your garden."

If they had indeed been dropped by a departing thief, she said - perhaps from a split sack, or stuffed hastily into a pocket - then they might mark his di-rection of travel.

"Two coins would be unreliable," she noted, "but three, in a straight line, might prove a useful clue."

But Pepys could not help. "'Twas my father who found them. You shall have to ask him, Abigail."

"How is your father?" Jacob asked, scrubbing at a grease stain on his waistcoat.

John Pepys was well into his seventh decade - his wife, Margaret, not much younger - and it showed. Stooped and forgetful, his ill health had concerned the inquisitors on their previous visit in September.

Pepys placed his elbows on the table and shook his weary head. "I fear for him, Jacob. I fear he may not have long left on God's earth. His strength is gone and his mind is feeble. The last time I was in Brampton, he set his shoes to roast in the oven."

"Then asking after the three coins might be...?" Jacob trailed off.

Pepys raised an eyebrow and gazed into the distance.

More ale arrived, and talk turned to the village they would revisit on the morrow.

Pepys had known Brampton since childhood. His father, born in neighbouring Cambridgeshire, had sent Samuel to Huntingdon Grammar School - where Oliver Cromwell had once been a pupil - even after the Pepyses moved to London.

There were other family connections to the area. The Brampton landowner was Lord Fairfax, whose mother was Pepys's great-aunt. Fairfax, an earl and admiral in the King's navy, had taken young Samuel under his wing, helping to advance him from minor clerical posts to his current exalted role as Clerk of the Acts.

John and Margaret Pepys's house in the village had been bequeathed to John by Robert Pepys, Samuel's uncle, who had served as Fairfax's bailiff.

"My name is spoken with care in Brampton," said Pepys, setting down his tankard with a satisfied sigh. "One word from me to my lord, and a man's standing might find itself... altered."

He appeared a tad tipsy.

"And Paulina?" Abby asked, a glint in her eye.

"Gah!" Pepys exclaimed. "The woman will drive me to Bedlam. Every time I find her a gentleman worthy of our family name, she declares him unfit to wed: ill-bred, too boring, too fond of ale..."

"What happened to Robert Endsum?" Abby asked, already knowing the answer, since Paulina had told her. "I thought you approved of him?"

"He died!" Pepys flung his arms in the air. "What am I to do?"

Dutifully, the inquisitors shook their heads.

Pepys leaned in. "Mark me, this latest suitor of hers..."

"Harry Packer," Abby obliged.

"Aye, Harry Packer. If that gull-groper bears no hand in the theft of my gold, I shall be mighty surprised."

"When last we visited Brampton, there was another in her affections," said Jacob.

"That oaf," muttered Pepys.

Abby eyed him over the rim of her tankard. "Will Farlow."

"Will Farlow! Aye. Returned to Huntingdon after the sorry Grimston affair, with his tail betwixt his legs. Where it belongs! He was not interested in Paulina, but in the Pepys name, and she would not see it."

Pepys, now breathing heavily, dabbed at his forehead with a lace handkerchief.

Downing her dregs, Abby gently nudged Jacob and nodded upstairs. It was time they took to their beds.

Abby tapped the table. "One final question, sir."

"Hmm, hmm, what is it, girl?" Pepys, slurring, surely needed his bed too.

"These rumours of the Wychwood Drummer. Where did they begin?"

Pepys tipped his tankard and realised the vessel was empty. With a splutter, he slapped it on the table. "In The Bull, would you believe? Where else do a village's tongues wag and half-truths breed, but its inn or tavern?"

Jacob, mindful of Abby's cue, rose and brushed again at the grease stain. It seemed to have grown. "I shall be glad to reacquaint myself with the inn, sir. I trust we will be staying there again. It was indeed a fine…"

Pepys raised a hand. "Ah," he said, eyeing the inquisitor. "I fear there is something I have not yet imparted to you."

Chapter Five

Return to Brampton

The coachman's bellowed "Whoa there!" drew the coach to a lurching halt outside the Pepys home in Brampton. It was an unscheduled stop on his route, but Mr Pepys was known to him, and had pressed an extra coin into his palm before they departed Stevenage.

Pepys was first out, peering up the garden path toward the two-storey dwelling with an expression of misgiving.

Abby, then Jacob, followed, stretching their aching limbs.

It was dark, cloud covering the moon, the only light flickering golden in the Pepyses' windows. Cold, too. Frost crunched beneath the inquisitors' feet, and their breath hung in clouds.

The air was still and quiet. Beyond the horses' snuffling and the unnerving cry of an owl, nothing stirred. So unlike London. Abby and Jacob were glad to have experienced Brampton's eeriness before.

It set Jacob on edge, his ears pricked for the sound of distant drumming.

Abby tugged at his sleeve. "Come," she said.

As they neared the front door, a face appeared pressed against the window, gaze shielded from above by a pale hand. With a muffled cry, it vanished, and the next moment John Pepys was at the door to greet his son.

"Paulina heard the coach," he said, grasping Samuel's hand. "What brings you to us again so soon?" Then, noticing Abby behind, his cheery disposition faltered. "Ah. Your inquisitor also. You're here for the gold, I take it?"

When Abby reached the door, John held her by the shoulders at arm's length. She was struck by how his long white shirt and brown waistcoat hung from his bony frame. His silver hair clung to his scalp in wisps.

He gazed upon her as if she were his own daughter. "Arabella Harford! My, how you've grown. Pray, enter, my dear. Enter. You are most welcome."

Jacob was next, already wondering what name the old man might bestow on him. *Jonas Sanders? Joseph Stanhope?*

"And who might you be?" John Pepys asked. "Strapping young fellow!"

Samuel accosted his father in the doorway, motioning for Abby and Jacob to precede him into the hall. There, seated at the long oak table the inquisitors had themselves used the previous September, were Margaret and Paulina Pepys.

Both women wore woollen coats against the cold, with aprons and coifs - Margaret's grey and unadorned, befitting her age, while Paulina's deep blue suggested a younger woman's vanity.

While Margaret smiled politely, Paulina leapt up and hugged Abigail. The two women - Paulina being a few years older - had not seen eye to eye in the early days of the witchcraft inquiry, but the ice had quickly thawed. Abby had saved her life, after all.

As had Jacob, though Paulina refrained from embracing him, having noticed her brother scowling.

"Will you sit?" she asked, pulling out a chair for Abby. Then she gestured to the playing cards scattered about the tabletop. "We were playing One-and-Thirty."

"Are you hungry?" Margaret Pepys asked.

Her son, eavesdropping, replied before Jacob could even open his mouth.

"Aye, Mother. Starved."

It sent Margaret shuffling into the kitchen, one hand pressed to the small of her back, murmuring apologies as she went.

The room was as Abby and Jacob remembered it: all oak beams and whitewashed plaster, small enough to bear an air of warmth even when the hearth was cold – though the new arrivals were glad to find it otherwise. There was none of the ostentation of their son's house, just a few modest ornaments upon the mantelpiece and the occasional rustic tapestry.

These folk lived within their means, which were not considerable. Besides Samuel's handouts, the household income depended upon rent from the inherited land and Paulina's work as a herbalist, concocting and selling remedies for common ailments.

"What brings you to Brampton?" Paulina asked as she tidied the playing cards.

The taut tone of her voice suggested she knew very well.

"Your brother's gold?" Abby replied softly.

Replacing the cards in their box, Paulina nodded to herself, just as her father and brother joined them.

She stood and allowed Samuel to kiss her on the cheek. The moment bore all the tenderness of a cattle sale.

"Sam's brought his inquisitors," John said, taking his seat at the head of the table. "Help find that gold." He winced.

"Their names are Abigail and Jacob, Father," Pepys said loudly.

"Aye, I know that!" John shot back. "And I'm not deaf, by the by."

Abby turned to him. "How have you been, Mr Pepys?"

"Sixty-five," John replied, pausing during the uncomfortable silence that followed, then grinned broadly. "I'm jesting with you, Arabella. I'm well, and obliged to you for asking."

His son rose angrily from his chair. "This is no laughing matter! A significant sum has been stolen from me - enough to pay for this place ten times over - and 'tis all your fault."

The old man's face crumpled. His furrows seemed to have multiplied in the few months since the inquisitors' previous visit. He wheezed as he breathed, and sat with a prominent stoop. The backs of his hands spoke of age.

Abby had to agree with her employer, that John Pepys did not seem long for this earthly realm.

"I could investigate the garden, if you wish?" Jacob piped up.

If he had thought it might appease his employer's sullen mood, he was sorely mistaken.

"An absurd idea!" Samuel snapped. "'Tis darker than the Devil's soul out there. We must hunt on the morrow. Until that time…" He trailed off and slumped back into his seat.

Abby leaned across and placed a hand on John's arm. He managed a smile.

"You found three coins?" she said. "Lying on the lawn?"

"That I did, 'tis true."

"Were they arranged, perchance, in a straight line?"

The old man gazed up into the rafters, as all present held their breath.

At length, he returned his gaze to Abby. "Aye, I do believe they were."

"Which way were they pointing, Mr Pepys?" she asked.

"Why, in the direction of Wychwood."

Beside her, Abby sensed Jacob tensing.

Chapter Six

Country Tales

S amuel Pepys folded his arms. "There are certain particulars of this terrible matter I have kept from you. It seemed prudent to allow you to discover them for yourselves, for your interpretation may differ from mine. This Wychwood tale being one of them."

Having reheated the family's mutton stew, Margaret Pepys returned to the hall, struggling under the weight of a large ceramic pot. Jacob leapt up to help, and shortly the three visitors were dipping torn chunks of Mistress Pepys's bread into the unctuous gravy.

"On your previous visit to Brampton, was there talk of the Watson family?" John Pepys asked the inquisitors.

When both regarded him blankly, he added, "Aye, they keep to themselves."

He went on to explain…

Some five or six years ago, Alexander Watson and his wife had lived in Brampton, in a cottage on Portholme

Meadow. He farmed pigs, while his wife, Sarah, was a midwife and healer. They had two young sons, Ned and Jack.

Even then, they were rarely seen in the heart of the village. Alexander had a propensity to rage, and was barred from The Bull. His wife, though trusted for her skills, was a timid woman with little to say for herself, which roused suspicion in a place where gossip and chatter were lifeblood.

Then one day, the pigs were gone and the cottage was found empty, of both Watsons and their possessions. Someone claimed to have seen Alexander driving his livestock into Wychwood.

It was later confirmed by a travelling tinker that the Watsons had indeed built themselves a hovel deep in the woods.

"'Twas said he'd stolen and butchered a neighbour's calf that harsh winter, and fled to avoid the magistrate," John said.

"'Tis not what I heard," his wife interjected. "I heard that Sarah cursed one of her salves, sent poor Mr Blakemore into a terrible fever, such as he near passed on. Witchcraft, they said."

Paulina buried her face in her hands at the mention of witchery. "Nay, Mother. Sarah delivered a stillborn child, but the mother swore she heard it cry out. That's what folk whispered."

Jacob raised an eyebrow and glanced at Abby. "Such are country tales, where fact and fancy dwell side by side."

Samuel sighed. "These country folk spin tales for want of livelier diversion."

"And their connection to the gold?" Abby asked John.

The old man knitted his brow. "Whose connection, lass?"

Hearing Samuel shift in his seat, Abby added quickly, "The Watsons. They're linked to your son's stolen hoard."

"Ah!" John exclaimed, as if hearing the notion for the first time. "The three coins?"

She nodded eagerly.

"Pointed the way to Wychwood. Moreover…"

"Moreover," Samuel cut in. "Two figures - young men, I heard tell - were seen one night, under cover of darkness, carrying heavy sacks from this very garden."

"Why were they not apprehended?" Jacob asked.

That silenced the room.

Abby caught her employer's eye. "What night was this?"

Samuel looked to his father. John Pepys had become distracted by a spider crawling up his arm, which he was trying to coax onto a finger.

With an exasperated sigh, Paulina came to his aid. "A week or more past. Father and Mother were visiting Dr Bramwell. I was at The Bull with Harry, served well by

Hatty all night. Since word spread of the three coins, our garden has been plagued by moonlight rogues digging up the lawn. We've had to take turns keeping watch at the window, to chase them away. 'Tis why we're all so exhausted."

Pepys clasped his puffy cheeks. "My gold, at the mercy of blackguards!"

"And these two young men carrying heavy sacks," Jacob said, "are said to be the Watson sons?"

Having transferred the spider to his finger, John now held it out, marvelling at the tiny creature dangling from a thread. "Aye, 'tis what I was told. The Drummer was heard that very night, deep within the forest, warning folk from Wychwood, guarding the hoard. Not been heard for many a year. Not since the Watsons first disappeared into Wychwood."

"And as well we know," Paulina added, shaking her chestnut hair, "there is nought Brampton folk dread more than the name Witch."

It was too much for Samuel to bear. "This is not about you!" he roared. Rising, he tore the periwig from his head and wrung it in his hands. His eyes flamed, his cheeks flushed, and his gaze bored into his sister. "I see you wear a new bracelet." His voice trembled with suppressed rage. "Is it silver?"

Paulina shrank back in her seat.

"I assume *he* gave it to you?" her brother pressed.

She managed the faintest of nods.

"And where, pray, did this idle suitor of yours find the money?"

Paulina's eyes narrowed, and she pulled herself upright. "Do you accuse my Harry of… of…?"

Hands raised in a gesture of peace, John struggled to his feet, joints cracking. His wife, who was apt to let the men speak, burrowed her chin into her chest, and seemed to wish she could disappear.

"I believe 'tis high time we all retired to our beds," said John, "ere one of us utter harsh words they may live to regret."

Abby and Jacob slept on the floor of the Pepyses' kitchen, which had retained some warmth from the oven. Samuel took his father's bed, the elder Mr Pepys sleeping beside his wife for the first time in… nobody could remember. Paulina slept alone.

As he was removing his first boot, Jacob heard movement in the garden and hastened outside in time to chase away three shadowy figures, who fled across meadowland toward the church.

They were too far off to warrant a chase. He stood there for a while, watching them recede into darkness, lost in the sense of space and the aching stillness. It was then that he heard it, very faint, from way across the fields: the insistent beat of a drum. A solemn tattoo, drawn out as if for the dead.

Rat-a-tat rat-a-tat rat-a-tat

Fear tingled at the nape of his neck, and he hurried inside.

"I heard it!" he cried, catching his breath.

Abby, who was combing her hair, yawned. "Heard what, Jacob?"

He caught her by the upper arms and shook her. "The Drummer! The Wychwood Drummer!"

Her mouth fell open. "Don't be…" But she could see it in his ashen face.

She might not trust tales of spirits, yet she trusted Jacob - and he had heard something very wrong out there.

She flung open the Pepyses' door and stood stock still, listening.

Jacob was right behind her. "From that dir…"

"Hush!" she urged.

The trees rustled and the wind sighed.

But the Drummer had fallen silent.

Chapter Seven

Second Son

Margaret Kight was no Londoner by birth. She was raised in Winchcombe in Gloucestershire, some hundred miles from the city. The town had once thrived on pilgrims and the wool trade, but by the early 1600s, when Margaret was born, folk were speaking of it as "a miserable poor place".

Her father, Richard Kight, a victualler and freeman, was known locally for his defiance of the Lord of the Manor. His children – Katherine, Lissett, Elenor, William and Richard, besides young Margaret – inherited some of that same spirit: restless, argumentative, keen to better themselves.

Like so many daughters of such households, Margaret migrated to London in her teens, among the stream of young women seeking wages and prospects in service. Through Gloucestershire connections she found work as a washmaid in the household of Lady Mary Vere in Clapton.

This was no lowly station. Lady Vere's servants learned not only the habits of a great house, but also absorbed the Puritan-

ical fervour that would later colour Margaret's arguments with her second son.

Margaret grew accustomed to the strict routines: prayers at dawn and dusk, plain meals taken in silence, Sundays devoted to scripture. She formed friendships among the other servants, young women like herself seeking betterment, and together they learned skills that would serve them well.

It was, she came to understand, the best a victualler's daughter could hope for – practical preparation for the day she might run her own home.

John Pepys was another migrant, though his path ran from Cottenham, north of Cambridge. His was a large family, with cousins spread across the Norfolk Fens and west to Huntingdon. These folk were of yeoman stock, neither gentry nor poor, but bound close enough to the soil to know hard labour and the need for steady trade. To John, that meant London.

He set himself up as a tailor, having served a four-year apprenticeship. Rejected by the Merchant Taylors' Company, one of the great livery guilds who set standard of workmanship, he was obliged to operate outside the City wall.

His rented house stood in Salisbury Court off Fleet Street, overlooked by St Bride's Church behind, its clamouring brass bells providing a rhythm to his day. Narrow-fronted, with jettied upper storeys leaning out above the street, its window displayed garments to catch the eye.

The business brought customers but few friends. Men came for alterations and fittings, discussed the cut of a doublet or the quality of wool, paid their few coins and departed. John found himself longing for the easy companionship of his Cambridgeshire cousins – the shared ales after harvest, the gossip on market day. Here, he was simply another tradesman among thousands, with little choice but to strive.

Through the door lay the shop-chamber: low-beamed, its shelves stacked with cloth, and a long looking glass on one wall, where patrons might admire their appearance in John's latest garb. Behind were the kitchen and yard, smoky from the spits, where tubs of ale and salted meat were stored.

Up a flight of stairs stood the cutting-room, with its long board for laying out cloth, drawers and presses, and truckle beds to be pulled out at night. Off this floor, the parlour offered a more orderly space, with leather chairs and a table for receiving guests.

Above again were the family chambers, with a modest adjoining study, where John kept his papers and sat by candlelight to keep his accounts. At the very top, in the garret beneath the eaves – stifling in summer, bitterly cold in winter – the children would sleep… When they arrived, God willing.

But first he would need a wife.

The streets outside milled with young men in gowns attending the nearby Inns of Court, and thumped and creaked with the sounds of printers and their presses. The Thames ran but a stone's throw away, calling to the assorted carts laden with goods clattering past, and when the wind blew westward, the stench of the Fleet Ditch assaulted the nostrils.

It was amid this maelstrom, moving in the same circles of eager tradesfolk, that John Pepys had the fortune to encounter Margaret Kight. She brought with her the grit of Winch-combe and the discipline of Her Ladyship's household; he, the steadiness of a craftsman who valued his worth, even if he might not achieve it. It was enough to set them courting.

John and Margaret wed on 15 October, 1626, when she moved into Salisbury Court and set about delivering children.

First came Mary in 1627, followed a year later by Paulina. For a while, it seemed that God was smiling, but grief would soon overshadow the family. Poor little Esther, born in 1630, was lost within a year, mere weeks before the arrival of Margaret's first son, John.

Midwives came and went, neighbours brought possets and broth, but sorrow clung to the walls even as Margaret busied herself with the household duties. With John lately baptised, already she was heavy with another child.

On the night of 23 February 1633, in the rooms above Salisbury Court, Margaret once more took to her bed, ag-onised and desperate. Candles guttered as the wind rattled through ill-fitting shutters, and from the street drifted the drunken cries of apprentices returning late from the taverns. On the floor below, John Pepys prayed.

This child, born at nine of the clock, clawing at the air, was carried that very night to the font at St Bride's, lest he too be lost. They named him Samuel.

Chapter Eight

In the Garden

The flagstone floor of the kitchen made for a fitful night's sleep. For longer than he cared to remember, Jacob had lain awake, eyes wide, hands behind his head, intent upon the nightly sounds of the countryside. Straining his ears for any malevolent crackle, until he swore he heard the Drummer once again.

When Abby stirred beside him, he could not be certain he had slept at all.

The bell of St Mary Magdalene, across a meadow from the Pepyses', chimed the sixth hour as they stepped outside. Margaret was in her kitchen, sparking kindling for the oven, and they could hear the two men upstairs discoursing in low tones.

Both Abby and Jacob were discomforted after sleeping fully clothed against the cold, and the fresh breeze on their faces felt cleansing. A few birds called from the hedgerows, the sky was bright if clouded, and the morning felt invigorating – in stark contrast to the brooding gloom of the previous night.

Following a stone pathway, they circled the house to the garden at the rear. The lawn was long and narrow, bordered by flower beds and herb gardens. The cherry trees at the far end were gnarled and bare, and the hedge border had a pleasing evergreen lustre. Off to one side stood the timber summerhouse, with its steeply sloping tiled roof, shuttered for the winter.

Everything was crusted with a layer of frost so thick, it might almost pass for snow.

Reaching the herbs, Abby plucked a lavender sprig between her thumb and forefinger, inhaling the scent. "Where do we look?"

Jacob shrugged. "If the man who buried the gold cannot find it, what chance have we?"

It was a fair point.

Mimicking Abby, he stooped to caress a leaf, then recoiled, furiously rubbing his fingers.

"That's a stinging nettle, you clodpot!" she exclaimed, laughing. "The bed needs weeding." Then she turned, surveying the garden. "The whole place needs some love."

As do I, thought Jacob sulkily.

His eye was caught by something near the cherry trees, and he loped toward it. "Look," he said, pointing to the ground. "Somebody has dug up the turf. No doubt those three scoundrels I chased off last night."

Abby joined him. "Did you see their faces?"

He sniffed the air. "'Twas too dark. Yet I wondered…"

"The Grimstons?"

"Indeed. There were three sons, were there not? Uncouth louts."

Abby replaced the unearthed sod and patted it down. "Doesn't mean it was them." She looked up at him, shading her eyes from the daylight. "Though you have to wonder."

They had first encountered the Grimstons last September, when the farmer, Godfrey "Goddie" Grimston, accused Paulina Pepys of witchcraft. Now his three sons were orphans, and might well harbour resentment towards the Pepys family after the inquisitors had cleared Paulina's name.

Not that any grievance was needed, Abby pointed out. "The lure of such a vast bounty is reason enough for theft."

Unnoticed, Samuel Pepys joined them.

A night's sleep seemed to have served him well. He appeared calm, and the blotchiness that had marked his face as he railed the previous night was gone. He had changed into a dark green embroidered waistcoat and matching doublet which, Abby thought, suited their rural surroundings rather well.

"How fare you, sir?" asked Jacob.

Pepys nodded curtly.

Abby glanced about the garden. "Where was it buried?"

Pepys let out a bitter laugh. "If only we knew! My father has forgotten, and Paulina claims likewise. His mind is clearly failing. Hers, on the other hand…" He pursed his lips. "I should never have entrusted them with such a sum."

Jacob reached a reassuring hand toward his employer's shoulder, thought twice, and pulled back. "We shall find your gold, sir."

"I pray you do, Jacob."

"Why did you not dig it up sooner?" Jacob added, and caught Abby's sigh. Still he ploughed on. "You feared the Dutch fleet, yet they never came. Nigh on a year has passed since."

Pepys planted his feet, his expression bordering on defiance. "Since, Mr Standish… Since…" He slumped. "I was foolish. I had no need of such a sum and thought it safest here, where none besides my closest kinfolk knew of its existence. Then, around Christmastime, whispers grew that something might be amiss - I know not from where. I should have acted sooner. Such an oaf."

Shortly, they were joined by John Pepys, and toured the garden together, pointing and provoking, hoping to reignite his memories of the burial night all those months ago. The old man only became increasingly flustered.

A limpid winter sun rose, and the frost began to melt, shimmering white turning to glistening green. The inquisitors could see the scars in the beds and turf, where diggers had thrust their spades. The entire garden, it seemed, had at some point been turned over.

It had crossed both their minds that the gold might be lost, rather than stolen - hidden somewhere obscure and resting there still, forgotten. Now it appeared that the despairing Pepyses, and later their nighttime invaders, had been thorough. The gold, most likely, was gone.

The four of them stopped at the summerhouse. John pushed open the door, and Abby and Jacob peered inside. Two upholstered chairs sat facing the shutters; garden tools - bill hook, spade, hoe and rake - were stacked against the timber walls, darkened with damp; and in one corner was a wooden chest bound with ironwork and padlocked.

John handed Jacob the key. "It has been searched," the old man said wearily. "More than once. And now lies…"

Jacob lifted the lid, Abby peering at his side.

"…empty."

Abby turned to John. "But the gold… Was it ever in there?"

He met her gaze with watery eyes. "An old fool, I may be, Abigail, but I would not hide treasure in a chest. It would be rather… obvious, do you not think?"

"And you made no note of the hiding place?"

John shot his son a guilty glance. "Ah," he said. "I do believe that I did."

"That, too, has slipped your memory?" Abby asked, trying to sound sympathetic.

"I never considered I would need it." He paused and shook his head. "I'm an old man, soon to be gathered to his fathers. My…"

Jacob hushed him with a raised palm. "Fear not, Mr Pepys. If there was a note made of the gold's whereabouts, I shall find it. I shall turn the house inside out, if necessary."

"Oh dear," murmured John.

Chapter Nine

Back at The Bull

Abby and Jacob set off toward The Bull, following a pathway that skirted the meadow behind the Pepyses'. Ahead rose the tower of the 13th-century Church of St Mary Magdalene. To its left stood the inn, its thatched roof - as Pepys had warned them - now gone, burned to ashes.

They would not lodge there this time, to their sorrow, for they had been warmly received before and had grown fond of the innkeeper and his wife.

The memories flooded back as they drew closer.

Behind the church, they remembered, lay the dingy stone lock-up where they were once imprisoned. They passed the cottage owned by Rebecca Thacker, the woman accused alongside Paulina Pepys of witchcraft. In the bitter aftermath, they had learned, she had left for Cambridge.

Further east, out of sight behind trees, lay the village hall and the magistrate, Bulstrode Bennett's house. West-

ward, across wintry fields, stood the Grimston household, and beyond that the Ravenscourt estate, its
sprawling manor house a mere speck in the landscape.

Jacob's eyes travelled south to where the estate
sloped into dense forest stretching to the horizon.

"Wychwood?" he asked, seeing Abby do the same.
She nodded pensively.

"What do you make of it all?" He asked.

Abby stopped, her expression troubled. "This may
be a case too far, Jacob. The only people we can trust -
the Pepyses - prove unreliable. Where does that leave
us? The Grimstons, the Watsons - we can expect short
shrift from them. And that's but the beginning."

Jacob gazed at the ground. "You say we can trust
the Pepyses, yet our Mr Pepys seems not to trust his
own sister. Already I feel uneasy about her suitor, that
Harry Packer, ere I have even set eyes on the fellow."

She grabbed his hand and spoke low, glancing back
towards the Pepyses'. "I took Paulina to one side last
night, when the men were upstairs preparing for bed.
She confessed to me, she didn't bury the gold with
John, but was away visiting… a friend."

"Then she knows nought of the gold's whereabouts?"

"So she told me."

"And would rather her brother thought her fee-
ble-minded…"

"Than admit she didn't help her father, and thus cared nought for his precious gold."

Jacob whistled. "We tread a fine line in our dealings here."

Abby set off again. "We do indeed."

He caught her up and grasped her shoulder. "You do trust me?"

She stopped again, hands on hips. "With my life, Jacob. Why would I not?"

The inn was a sorry sight.

All that remained of the roof was a tangle of collapsed, charred beams. The stone walls still held firm, and the chimney stacks rose scorched against a saffron morning sky. The windows on the upper floor, where Abby and Jacob had slept, were gone, the painted stonework around them singed and blackened.

Yet the tap-room still functioned, Pepys had assured them, the villagers having acted in time to douse the flames on the ground floor. A storm had passed by as they toiled, opening the Heavens, and many praised the Lord himself that the damage was not more severe.

Jacob tried the door and found it locked, while Abby peered in through a window.

"All quiet," she said. "Let's venture round the back."

One of the storage huts there had been reduced to charred stumps, likely from falling debris, yet the remainder stood unharmed. Behind one, they spotted Hatty. Kneeling with her back to them, she was digging into a low mound of raised earth with a trowel. It was a grave, marked with a tilting wooden cross, upon which was scratched a name: *RUSTY*.

Both inquisitors remembered the inn's dog, ever beside their table hunting for scraps – until its untimely demise.

"You loved that creature," Abby said.

Hatty let out an almighty shriek, dropped the trowel as if it were scorched, and swivelled. Her eyes widened as recognition flooded her face.

"I-I was just planting flowers for poor Rusty," she stammered.

Then, slapping her thigh, she pushed herself upright with a grunt. Ruddy-cheeked and matronly, she looked in fine fettle despite the recent troubles, her untied chestnut curls falling loose about her shoulders.

"Mistress Harcourt and Mr Standish! Well I never did!" She crushed them both in the same embrace, before stepping back. "What brings you here? Not more witches, I do 'ope?"

"Gold," said Jacob. "Stolen gold."

Hatty's hand flew to her mouth. "I heard tell," she said hoarsely. "Your dear Mr Pepys. 'Tis a sorry state of affairs when a gentleman's hard-won riches are taken from him in the dead of night."

"Where's Barty?" Abby asked.

"Still clearin' out the mess from the fire." The words caught in her throat.

"Abby! Jacob!" Barty Nettlewood came into view up a dirt track, dragging an old hand cart, wheezing noisily. "Well, bless my soul!"

Jacob rushed forward and took the cart from him. It was blackened with soot and strewn with broken staves and charred wood.

The innkeeper, who was considerably shorter than Jacob, patted him on the hip. "There's a good fellow," he said, wiping his hands on a tatty apron.

"Where's your eyepatch?" Abby asked, recalling the comic prop Barty had worn when last they met.

"I fear," he puffed, still gathering breath, "I may have looked somewhat the ass."

They hugged, the affection genuine. The innkeeper looked tired, eyes dark-rimmed, with scrapes and cuts upon his grimy arms.

He saw them notice, smiled weakly, and pointed to the ravaged building. "'Tis back-breaking toil," he said. "Yet what choice do we have?"

As he beckoned them inside through the rear door, some of his customary good humour returned. "You must forgive the hole in the roof," he said with a wry laugh.

All that remained of the ceiling was a lattice of blackened beams sturdy enough to withstand the fire, upon which fresh timbers had been laid to create a makeshift covering.

Barty bustled to his counter. "Pray, be seated," he said, rubbing his hands in glee. "Oh, it does my heart good to see you both."

Hatty darted ahead of them, wiping a table with a cloth.

"You're staying, then?" Jacob asked. "Despite the fire."

Hatty looked across to Barty. "I fear not," she said, scrunching the cloth in her hands. "Too many memories turned to ash. We'll repair it as best we can ere we depart."

"We've kin arriving with carts a few days hence, help us carry our things away," Barty added.

Abby gave a small shake of her head. "Such a shame."

Hatty sighed. "The Lord gives, and the Lord takes away." Then she brightened, forcing a smile. "We'll be delighted to serve you both till then. 'Twill be our pleasure."

And off she trotted to her kitchen.

The fire had broken out three nights ago, the inquisitors learned. The acrid odour of its aftermath still lingered. The whitewashed walls bore a pale-grey smear where soot had been scrubbed away, and the flagstone floor was scattered with stray lumps of debris.

Yet the tap-room furniture appeared largely unharmed, and the staircase, though scorched, still stood. Barty's counter, with its piled barrels, appeared spotless as he busied himself pouring ales.

When he joined them at a table, settling beside Jacob with a grunt, he raised his tankard.

"To The Bull that ne'er shall perish!"

It was a bittersweet moment for Abby and Jacob as they supped, recalling the inn smelling of hops and tobacco, and laughter echoing about its walls.

"Pray tell us what happened," Abby said when Hatty joined them, settling opposite her husband.

"Aye, who set the fire?" Jacob added.

Hatty shook her head grimly, fixing Barty with a stare. "Who started that blaze, Bartholomew Nettlewood?"

He squinted.

Without warning, his wife was off her stool, jabbing a finger. "He started it, didn't 'e, useless lump! I kept telling 'im to sweep out them chimneys."

Barty's mouth sagged open.

She retook her seat, arms folded, glaring. "Aye, you did, you great oaf! Think on!" She swung toward Abby. "'Next 'e'll swear 'e's not responsible for our children. But I tell you 'e is - and I should know."

Abby caught Jacob's eye.

"Then 'twas not arson?" he ventured. That was what Mr Pepys had said.

Hatty took a long swig of her ale.

Barty dropped his gaze, then lifted it again. "Since you were last in Brampton, such was the turmoil over them witches, and we," he nodded toward his wife, "granted you shelter…"

"Some folks have took against us," Hatty cut in.

Jacob adjusted his periwig. "Since you granted us shelter? Are we…"

"Unpopular?" Hatty interjected. "I'd say so!"

"Many considered the justice meted out by the Senior Magistrate righteous," Barty added. "Yet others did not. They still believe the Pepys and Thacker women to be witches."

"Then Brampton is divided?" Abby said.

"More so, since the Drummer returned." Hatty shuddered and tapped the table sharply. "I heard it first, didn't I? Laughed at me, 'e did - till he heard it too. Next thing, all the village knows, and everyone's up in arms!"

Jacob furrowed his brow. "The village is divided enough to burn down this inn?"

Hatty gave a rueful snort. "I still maintain it was 'im. Hasn't cleaned out them chimneys these past ten years." She drew herself up. "But mark me: we'll leave this inn as proud as when we arrived."

Folk began to drift through the door, seeking breakfast and ale. Many looked to be farm labourers, taking their first rest since dawn. Each one appeared to cast the inquisitors a look, as if placing their faces, and more than one lip curled into the ghost of a snarl.

Or had they imagined it?

Their previous inquiry had ended in the village hall, under the gaze of every soul in Brampton. They were known here and, it now appeared, not entirely welcome.

Barty returned to his counter, while Hatty vanished into her kitchen, keen for the villagers' coin. As the tables filled, the murmurs grew, low and restless.

The inquisitors shrank into their seats. Whenever their eyes strayed about the tap-room, they found others' fixed on them still.

"I don't like it here," hissed Jacob, leaning across the table.

"Neither I, Jacob. But what can we do?"

"We can leave!"

She drew closer. "Flee our first battle? I thought you braver than that."

He snapped back, snatching up his tankard.

Hatty returned with two bowls of hot posset, and set them down.

"Where will you move to?" Abby asked, hoping it passed for easy discourse.

"Don't want no witch-folk here," came the growl.

Hatty wheeled on the fellow, wizened and sneering.

"You mind yer own business, Robert Rance," she scolded him. "And the rest of you." She tapped the table lustily. "These fine folk are our guests."

Like chastened children, the gathered men returned to their breakfasts.

Hatty turned to Abby. "Perhaps to my sister's in the north. She..."

"Stole away by night, as might the godless," Rance muttered.

Hatty's head snapped round. "You're in my house now, tattler - mind yer tongue."

Rance raised an eyebrow. "Just sayin'."

"Well don't."

Lips pursed, Hatty returned her attention to the inquisitors. "My young sister, Dotty, left Brampton some years ago, poor girl, hounded by plain lies. Such is this place. You've seen it for yourselves - the foul slanders folks cast." She gazed from face to face, but all ignored her. At length, she breathed out sharply. "What of you two? Where will you stay, now we can offer no bed for the night? With the Pepyses?"

Jacob frowned. "Their house is too small, or so we were told."

"Mr Pepys wishes us to spend the nights in Wychwood," Abby added. "We..."

A chair scraped, and hush fell.

Robert Rance was on his feet, stooped in a tattered black coat, resembling an old crow. "The Drummer returns," he said with a gap-toothed leer.

Another man rose toward the rear of the tap-room, hat brim low. "The Drummer appeared as the Watsons were banished to Wychwood, then fell silent. Now he returns - and why? Evil spirits are abroad since the witch-finder visited this place, you mark me, and William Rudd will have his justice."

"Nonsense, 'tis the gold the Drummer wants," someone piped up.

A few nodded approval. "He guards it well," said one.

"Aye," Rance added. "The gold. You want to know who thieved it, look no further than them Watsons, scaring folk from Wychwood. Why? 'Cos they've secrets to hide. Remember them Watson lads was seen, weighed down with sacks, skulking from the Pepys place."

With that, he finished his dregs, tossed a coin on the table and headed for the door.

When it closed, Hatty muttered to herself, "Don't trust them Watsons."

"You see them here?" Abby asked.

"Not if I can help it. Had to bar the husband. Some temper on 'im."

Jacob beckoned her closer. "How is it that all know of Mr Pepys's hoard?" he said quietly.

"Seen burying it, wasn't he?" a voice called.

"Pish!" came another. "The physician let it slip. Drunk, he was, rowing with that strumpet of his."

"I blame them Grimstons," another cut in. "They…"

"*Silence!*" bellowed Hatty, loud enough that Barty ducked behind his counter. "I'll have no slanderous gossip in here!"

"Always a first time," came the reply.

Chapter Ten

Spare a Farthing

Both Abby and Jacob exhaled with relief as The Bull's door closed behind them. Jacob bent, hands on knees, and was about to speak when Abby drew him away, up the westward path toward Ravenscourt Manor.

"We mustn't let them hear," she said, once they were safely out of earshot. "Thank the Lord we're staying in Wychwood."

Jacob pulled on his hat brim. "Ne'er did I think I would agree with you, but aye. Brampton seems a nest of rum devils. Even the Nettlewoods grow tense."

Nuns' Meadow lay to their left, Portholme to their right, both wreathed in silvery-white. A stiff breeze blew, making the chill bite hard, tingling their ears and numbing their noses.

The fields were bare, the farmers having taken in their livestock. The great sails of the windmills on the slopes were turning. Though the corn was long since harvested, the miller's trade went on, grinding the last of the stored wheat and rye, and malt for winter ale.

They knew the road, having taken it before. The stile up ahead, beneath the oak, signalled the path south to the Grimstons' farmhouse. A mile or so farther on, they would come upon Nun's Bridge, crossing the Ouse, and the grand gatehouse of the Ravenscourt estate.

It was there they would find the physician, Archibald Bramwell, and his lover - secret lover, until the inquisitors had intervened - the stablemaid, Alice Wilkins. The two had been mentioned, among so much other spurious gossip, back at The Bull, which both Abby and Jacob had noted.

Behind them, St Mary Magdalene's bell echoed, and they counted the chimes: eleven.

They had tarried too long at the inn, hoping for clues, and had come away with a sackful of superstitions. Why, at one stage, the Rance fellow claimed to have seen the Wychwood Drummer with his own eyes - "Horns, he had, and cloven hooves, with wings and a forked tail" - yet when pressed, stammered and admitted it was too dark to see clearly.

It reminded Abby of what Mr Pepys had said: "These country folk spin tales for want of livelier diversion."

Who, then, to trust?

Their original plan had been to make their way to Wychwood while daylight remained. Neither relished finding their way through there after nightfall. Each had packed a satchel in readiness.

They were to lodge in an abandoned almoner's cottage, once part of the 11th-century Benedictine nunnery granted to Richard Cromwell after Henry VIII's dissolution of the monasteries. These days the estate belonged to Lord Fairfax, Pepys's benefactor, who had given leave for their use of the cottage.

Pepys had drawn them a crude map, which looked wholly insufficient.

Jacob blew into his cupped hands, watching the cloud of breath disperse through his fingers. "Where now?"

"I say we pay the physician a visit. According to that old man at The Bull, the talk of gold began with him."

"The same old man told us Mr Pepys himself was spied burying it, which we know cannot be true, since the task was entrusted to his father."

Abby smirked. "'Twas two different men telling those tales, Jacob."

Snatching up his satchel, he strode off on his long legs.

"Wait for me," she called after him.

He did not stop.

Jacob surely slowed his pace, however, as he approached the stile beneath the oak, its lowest bough hanging over the road like a draped arm.

To his left, a dirt path followed a dry-stone wall down through fields of frosted stubble, where, last September, they had seen Goddie Grimston and his sons rolling sheaves of corn.

Goddie had charged him, knocking him to the ground. His sons had gathered around him, one brandishing a sickle, another a flail, and together they had chased him away.

What could he have done, unarmed, against such numbers?

Goddie might be gone, but those swaggering sons remained, and were, Jacob felt convinced, the same figures he had seen fleeing the Pepyses' garden.

Perching awkwardly on the narrow step of the stile, keen to appear at ease, he watched Abby as she caught up.

Something about her gait annoyed him. It seemed mannered, not gay with abandon as she had been when first they trod this same road. He remembered her by Nun's Bridge, skipping ahead, then turning and laughing - the gradual unfolding of their friendship as they grew familiar with one another. He had chased her then. Such amusement.

Now, she seemed to swagger, arms swinging like a soldier's, chin raised. She had developed ideas above her station, and he blamed the theatre. Too much adulation could turn a head. Even one as measured as Abby's.

"A farthing for your thoughts," she said when she reached him.

"Why do you ask?"

"You seem… pensive."

"I am allowed to think, am I not? Or must all the thinking be yours?"

She screwed up her face. "What's wrong with you today? Have I said something to displease you?"

He licked his lips, sighed, and pointed down the pathway to a single-storey stone building with a thatched roof some way ahead. Thick grey smoke drifted from its chimney.

"The Grimstons?" she asked, rubbing her cheek nervously. "Aye, they trouble me also, but I say we wait. Of all the welcomes we may expect here, theirs will likely be the coldest."

He stood, face set. "And I say we confront them."

She stared back, part challenge, part puzzlement.

Seconds passed in silence, broken by the haunting call of a far-off wood pigeon.

"Very well," she said with a shrug. "Lead the way."

"You are to accompany me?" He slid off the stile, stumbling as he landed.

"We're partners, are we not? Mr Pepys's personal inquisitors?"

Had he misjudged her? "It may be dangerous. The last time we met, they attacked me. I should…"

She folded her arms. "If you go, I go."

He glanced down the pathway. "Then let us postpone the dread meeting. The Grimstons can wait." Brampton's chill had set him on edge, he realised. "We shall make for… Where are we making for?"

"The physician, Bramwell, lives on the Ravenscourt estate, on the way to Wychwood. Let's pay him a visit first."

Chapter Eleven

Edgar

Though he would not admit it, Jacob feared Lord Fairfax more than he did three rampaging Grimston lads. Fairfax held an exalted place in the King's navy.

Jacob had served also, as an apprentice purser at Greenwich dockyard, thankfully on dry land. His late father, Sir Miles, Surveyor to the Navy Board, had secured the post for him.

The apprenticeship had not lasted long, before he was dismissed for his umpteenth miscalculation, one that had put men's lives at risk.

Afterwards, he had moped about Standish Hall, gnawed by the shame, until his mother had grown weary of his long face and banished him to the family's townhouse on Strand Lane. He might still be dragging his heels, idle and feckless, had Mr Pepys not honoured his father's deathbed wish that Pepys take Jacob under his wing.

What if Fairfax knows of my blunders? he wondered. *How pathetic I should seem.*

Men wielding such power intimidated him, and His Lordship was another matter entirely. It all felt far too close to home.

The wide River Ouse lay frozen, its banks lined with weeping willow, beech and oak, their branches bare and skeletal. The bridge was stone with five arches, broad enough for horse and cart. After it, the road joined George Street which led to the county town of Huntingdon. Instead, they would veer left, toward the manor house.

Halfway across, Jacob stopped dead. "Did you feel that?"

She was lagging – as ever, with their mismatched strides – and caught him up. "Feel what?"

He stood rigid, eyes darting. "I… I felt a sudden chill pass through me, as though… I cannot explain it."

She took his hands in hers. They were icy cold. "Don't let this place unnerve you. I sense it too, Jacob – something in the air. Something awry. The sooner we retrieve the gold and leave for London, the better."

With an uncertain nod, he let her lead him from the bridge.

Not far ahead lay the Ravenscourt Estate gatehouse.

"Well," she said with a wry smile.

Their eyes were drawn to the twin carved sentinels flanking the main arch. These were no king's guards, but visions from a heathen past.

"Wodewoses," she said, recalling the old English name. "Wild Men."

They were tall, clad in armour hewn from rippling bark, with long faces and longer beards. Each clutched a stripped tree trunk in place of a staff, gazing imperiously over the land.

Abby and Jacob had passed them before, yet paid them little heed.

This time, the Wild Men had stopped them in their tracks.

"By night, I'll warrant they walk," said Jacob. "And I have no wish to meet them when they do so."

To their left, something flitted among the undergrowth, and both started.

"Heavens!" Abby gasped, clutching at her racing heart, then cast Jacob a reassuring grin. "Let's hope the physician has no surprises for us."

Ravenscourt Manor towered above them, its bay windows the height of a warehouse door. Above the crenellated roofline rose further rooftops, as if the estate went on forever.

Both lingered on the driveway, gazing at the main door, reluctant to knock. Beside them, the ornamental lawn and its manicured topiary shivered in the breeze; beyond lay barren and withered flower beds which, in summer, would blaze with colour.

Here, too, lay that unnerving sense of stillness.

"You should knock, Jacob," Abby said.

He knew it was true. Anything else would be untoward, weak-willed.

Am I weak? he wondered.

His surprisingly bold rap on the heavy oak assured him otherwise.

They recognised the servant at once. He had answered the door to them before.

Edgar.

The word *lugubrious* might have been invented for him.

Upright, like a beanpole - all the better to look down from - his tone carried a resigned disappointment.

"How may I assist you?" he drawled, a twitch of one eyelid suggesting he remembered them too.

Jacob spoke up. "We are…"

"I *know* who you are, sir," Edgar cut in. "His Lordship is expecting you."

Jacob turned to Abby, panic all over his face.

Edgar tapped him on the shoulder, and he turned back.

"By which I mean, sir, that His Lordship anticipated your arrival." The servant arched a groomed eyebrow.

"He has no desire whatsoever to make your acquaintance."

"Oh, thank Heavens for that!" Jacob blurted out, grinning like a fool. Then his expression fell. "I mean…"

"I know precisely what you mean, sir," Edgar intoned.

They stood there awhile, appraising one another.

"His Lordship informs me you are to reside in the almoner's cottage in Wychwood." The servant cleared his throat. "He did request that you remove your footwear upon entry."

Jacob cocked his head. "Our employer, Mr Pepys, told us it was abandoned, that we should expect it to be in a state of some decay."

"That may be so. Nevertheless, His Lordship requests that you remove your footwear upon entry."

Jacob smiled.

The servant lifted his nose a little higher. "Would you wish me to accompany you to Wychwood? His Lordship requested I guide you to his cottage."

Another second in Edgar's company, and Jacob felt he might explode. "Nay, I assure you, that will not be necessary… Edgar. Mr Pepys drew for us a map."

The eyebrow went again, accompanied by a proffered hand.

Resolutely to Jacob's rear, Abby rifled through her satchel and held out the map.

The servant inspected it, his disdain palpable.

"Indeed," he sniffed, handing it back, then under his breath added, "Should you wish to find yourself in Cambridge."

"What was that?" Jacob asked.

Abby stepped forward. "We'd be most grateful if you'd show us to the cottage, Edgar. But for now, we intend to visit Dr Bramwell."

Edgar bowed. "As you wish, mistress. You know the way, I believe."

The door closed.

Chapter Twelve

Heal Thyself

Skirting the manor house, the inquisitors found Archibald Bramwell's quarters in the rear wing. The physician was retained by Lord Fairfax to maintain his family's health, having overseen the births of His Lordship's ten children - all of whom had survived infancy.

It was no mean feat, and Bramwell's services were much sought after by those who could afford his fees.

Abby and Jacob had questioned him during their witchcraft investigation. Now they returned to him as a suspect.

Jacob remembered the fellow with distaste. Bramwell had flirted openly with Abby while treating him as if he were invisible. He was aloof and condescending, and Jacob quietly hoped he was guilty of the theft.

"Jacob!" Abby's voice caught in her throat. "I fear Dr Bramwell is dead."

Having rapped on the door with no response, then discovered it locked, she had pressed her face to the stained-glass window.

"He's in an armchair, not moving," she said, still staring. "His face… looks slack."

There came a *thump*, as Jacob drove his shoulder against the door. And again.

On the third attempt, splintering wood gave way, and Jacob vanished through the doorway, followed by a crash and the tinkling of broken glass.

"I am inside," he called.

She entered warily, taking in the scene.

Beyond the havoc Jacob had wrought, upending a table covered in jars and bottles, the room was in disarray. Papers lay scattered across the floor, a couple of paintings hung at wild angles, and Bramwell's desk and chair had been tipped over.

Jacob picked himself up, inspecting his palms for fragments of glass, and nodded to himself when he found none. Spilt powders and dried herbs had transferred themselves to his coat, and he dusted himself down.

"Was there a fight here?" he asked.

Abby knelt beside Bramwell, checking for a pulse, knowing she would find none. The physician lay slumped, arms dangling limp, mouth open, tongue lolling.

His wrist was cold.

"He's been dead some time," she said.

"How long?"

"I've no idea. You'd have to ask a physician."

Neither laughed.

"More's the point," she added. "Who murdered him?"

Jacob rubbed at a stubborn yellow stain on the knee of his breeches.

Abby cast her gaze about the room. "What do we know about Archibald Bramwell?" she wondered aloud.

"He thought himself handsome."

Raising her eyes, she tutted. "Remember your duty."

It was Jacob who first fixed upon the cause of death, which had been staring them both in the face.

"His throat looks red," he pointed out.

They found a leather belt concealed beneath a slew of papers beside the physician's armchair. Jacob held it against the angry band about Bramwell's neck, and the two appeared to match.

Since the physician was already wearing a belt, they assumed the assailant had whipped off their own to strangle the poor fellow. It would explain his bloodshot eyes and ghastly expression.

Though each inquisitor thought it, neither cared to voice it: *Archibald Bramwell looked as if he had seen a ghost.*

Abby busied herself searching the bookshelves for clues, while Jacob righted the physician's desk and chair, and sifted through his notes.

Bramwell's library rivalled Mr Pepys's in size and was no less weighty in subject matter. Some of the leather-bound volumes were so heavy that Abby staggered retrieving them from the shelves.

Among them were several by the controversial Nicholas Culpeper - *The English Physician*, *A Directory for Midwives*, *A Physical Directory* - derided among his peers, Abby had learned, since he treated the poor for free. Yet Bramwell was clearly a willing student.

Most of the texts were in Latin, which she had never been taught (a woman of her low means being unduly fortunate to read English). *Universa Medicina*, *Methodus Medendi*, *Claudii Galeni Opera Omnia*, *Avicennae Opera Omnia*… While most were battered, bent and dusty, Bramwell's copy of *Magni Hippocratis Coi Opera Omni*, by Hippocrates, looked all but new and unread.

Abby riffled the pages, looking for hidden notes, but found only scrawled questions and theories, on medical subjects beyond her.

Sighing, she looked to Jacob, who was poring over a thick notebook, his nose all but touching the pages.

It occurred to her that she had never seen him reading a book. "What have you found?"

"His casebook, dating from…," he turned back to the first page, "March 1658. It records his patients and the times he met with them, yet also personal asides steeped in self-doubt. Bramwell was not the cocksure figure he presented."

Abby was beside him in an instant, and slid the book from his hands. He stared, confounded, as she flicked through the pages, too absorbed to notice his indignation.

"'Arrived at the Ravenscourt estate,'" she read aloud. "'If it pleases the Lord, I believe I shall flourish here. I pray it shall be so.'"

Bramwell's hand was small, his letters meticulously formed, in a flowing style that pleased the eye and made his words easy to decipher.

"His visits have been few and far between of late," Abby said, flicking through pages toward the back of the book.

"Aye, I noticed also. Since the witchcraft hearing, it seems."

Abby gazed upwards. "When word spread of his trysts with the stablemaid, Alice Wilkins, some must have turned against him. 'Twould have lowered his standing in their eyes."

"I found…" Jacob tried to wrest the book from Abby, but she resisted.

"Tell me what you found, Jacob."

He took a deep breath. "I found mention of the visit of John and Margaret Pepys, for the trial of their sight, at ten of the clock in the night, on Monday January the fourth. The following day, he was visited by that suitor of Paulina's: Harry Packer."

She leafed through the thick yellow pages, stopped and read intently.

One page caught her eye – an entry had been circled several times. "He writes: 'M tells me the old woman's fevered secrets. Dare I act?'. Dated September 1666, when last we were here." She paused. "Who is this 'M', and what did she tell?"

"He knew something of the witches?"

"Or of the gold?"

While she was lost in thought, Jacob snatched the book back. "There is more," he said. "Watch."

Placing the tome spine-down on the desk, he allowed it to fall open. In the crease between the opened pages was the ragged stub of a leaf, torn close to the binding.

"A page has been ripped out," he said, somewhat smugly. "From April 1660."

"Excellent, Jacob!" she said, inspecting the stub.

Previously, her praise would have delighted him; today, it made him sniff.

He tightened, inhaled the air again, and peered about the room.

"What is it?" she asked.

"Can you not smell it?" He dropped, gazing about the floor. When he rose, he was clutching a glass decanter, a thumb of brown liquid remaining at its base.

He sniffed at the top. "Rum."

"Where's the cup?"

They both hunted about the floor but found nothing.

"Was he drinking from the decanter itself?" Jacob asked.

His query hung in the air.

As it did so, a loud crashing sound came from elsewhere in the apartment, causing both inquisitors to freeze.

"There's somebody in the house!" Abby cried, slapping the book shut and tucking it under her arm.

Jacob raced from the room, banging his head on the low doorway as he did so, with Abby hot on his heels. They found themselves in a wood-panelled hallway with two doors opposite, each slightly ajar.

Jacob barged through the first, to find Bramwell's kitchen. The hearth was cold, a solitary stool set before it. There were shelves on the walls, lined with jars and pewter, and a lone oak cupboard. A wicker basket rested on the table in the centre of the room, containing a loaf and protruding root vegetables.

As Abby joined him, she fond herself remembering the pot of Chinese tea Bramwell had brewed for them - her first taste of the exotic drink.

Jacob pushed her aside, making for the other door. When he opened it, he paused, then hastened in.

Abby found him at an open window, a shattered vase at his feet, having been knocked from an adjacent side-table. He peered through the window, left then right, and once again for good measure, before pulling himself back into the room.

"Whoever it was," he said, "they have escaped."

A blast of wintry air caught one of the shutters, sending it flying open, sweeping across the table where the vase had sat.

"Or our murderer is long gone," Abby said, "having left the window open behind them."

Jacob slammed the shutter closed. Having done so, he plucked a narrow shred of linen, pale and frayed, from the catch.

He held it up for Abby to see. "Torn from an apron in haste?"

This was Bramwell's chamber, a stout four-poster bed with cream drapes dominating the room. Elsewhere stood a carved chest, a washstand and a small writing table, all in meticulous order. On the table were two miniature portraits of a man and woman, both old, with kindly eyes.

Jacob paused at them, as if some trace of familiarity stirred, then moved to the chest.

Abby peered under the bed. Reaching in, she pulled out a rumpled dark cloak that smelled of the hearth, and tossed it to one side.

Jacob tried the lid of the chest and found it unlocked.

Abby joined him, lifting out a pair of buckled shoes. She set them aside with a couple of shirts, then dug deeper, fingers flicking through coats, shifts and stockings.

"Nought," she said when she reached the bottom, replacing the shirts and shoes on top.

Jacob heaved the chest onto its front and watched as the physician's clothes tumbled onto the floor.

Abby held her hand to her mouth.

"Bramwell is beyond caring," he said curtly. "I found a chest such as this at Franny Jenkins's lodgings in The Cock on Bow Street," he added, referring to their previous investigation off Drury Lane. "Her secrets were concealed at the very base."

She waited, tapping a foot, as he scrabbled through the spilt garments, feeling along hems and seams, growing more impatient as each search came to nought.

At length, he was forced to admit defeat. He could feel her eyes on him as he carelessly bundled the clothes back inside. Finally came the shoes, one in each hand.

He was about to set them down when he paused, weighing left against right.

"Hold," he said.

As he tipped the left shoe, a leather pouch slid into view.

Smiling slyly at her, he opened it and shook the contents into his outstretched palm.

There lay four golden broad pieces. So new did they look, they appeared to glow.

All were dated 1656; Cromwell in profile, laurel-crowned on one side, and a shield beneath a crown on the other.

Abby picked one out almost reverentially. She had seen Mr Pepys with gold coins, many times, but had never held one herself. It weighed heavy in her hand.

Around both edges ran inscriptions in Latin.

"What do they mean?" she asked Jacob, who had been schooled in Latin and Greek from an early age.

He winced; so little of it had stuck.

On the Cromwell side, following the word 'OLI-VAR', ran a string of letters meaningless to him. The reverse bore the legend 'PAX QVAERITVR BELLO'.

He scratched at his periwig. "Peace is sought through war?" he ventured, hardly confident.

Abby shook her head. "What a piece of work is a man," she said quietly.

He took the coin back, slipped all four into the pouch, and pushed it into the pocket inside his coat.

Abby gawped. "That's theft!"

"They are Mr Pepys's, and I shall return them to him. Anyhow," he tapped Bramwell's casebook, jutting from beneath her arm. "Are you keeping that?"

A glint lit her eyes. "Look," she said, allowing the book to fall open as Jacob had done. "This stub. What catches your eye?"

Among the garbled words that remained, some torn in half by the missing page, little made sense. Most seemed to deal with tinctures and trifling ailments.

Yet her gaze was drawn to one particular section. She pointed.

son present,
of child,
at hand. Agreed
t have I done?

"That final line," she said. "It surely reads, 'What have I done?' Whose child is that, and what was agreed, that Bramwell later deemed the page too perilous to keep?"

Chapter Thirteen

On Edge

Ravenscourt Manor had always seemed so sedate. Each time the inquisitors stood at the great door, the hallways within were silent, not a soul in sight, as if the house were abandoned.

Once they informed Edgar of Bramwell's death, servants poured from every corner of the estate. Lord Fairfax himself swept past them with a sidelong glance, resplendent in velvet and lace, his retinue bowing and scraping in his wake.

They watched them disappear as Edgar led them south through the ornamental gardens, in the direction of Wychwood.

The servant, in his forest-green livery with white silk breeches and high black boots, kept a punishing pace, on strides that rivalled Jacob's. His tall felt hat, its brim upturned, bore a band of Fairfax green.

He carried both inquisitors' satchels, which appeared not to burden him.

No one spoke. Birds circled above as they grew entranced by their own laboured breathing.

Passing through orchards, the trees fruitless and spindly, they emerged onto frozen meadowland sloping toward dense forest.

Abby, struggling to keep up, called out, "Edgar! Pray hold!"

He stopped and looked back, tutting under his breath.

Keen to rest, she asked, "What know you of Wychwood?"

That eyebrow lifted again. "I assume you wish to learn whether I have encountered the Wychwood Drummer?" The slightest of smiles curled his lips - the first sign of a heart they had witnessed. "I have. We all hear it at the manor, blown on the wind from the depths of Wychwood. Like a devil's spirit loosed upon the air."

"When did the drumming begin?" Abby asked.

"Many years ago. I have served His Lordship but these past two, and heard the unholy tattoo myself only last night." Noticing Jacob's glance to Abby, he continued, "I live in fear now. My colleagues who recall the Drummer from old tell me his beat has grown malicious - that he yearns to take our souls in our beds. I pray the Lord keeps me safe."

Edgar's jaw was clenched. He meant every word.

Jacob wrung his hands. "Have you… Have you *seen the spirit?*"

The servant's eyes hollowed. "Enough questions."

Abby and Jacob glanced at one another. Each had grown a little paler.

The closer they drew to Wychwood, the slower Edgar's pace became, until Abby could walk beside the two men with ease. Yet their mood was far from easy.

The winter sun seemed eager to flee, and mist crept over the land. The countryside turned ominous, and a single crow called from within Wychwood, its cry plaintive and unnerving.

From Brampton village, the church bell rang the third hour, each chime tolling as if for the dead – one for each of them.

They stopped at the forest edge. A narrow mud path cut between clustered tree trunks, disappearing into near darkness.

"Light your torches," Edgar told them, his tone clipped.

Abby and Jacob looked at one another, then at Edgar.

He groaned. "Clodpots. You brought no torches?"

The further Edgar went from the great house, Abby thought, the more he changed.

"How do you expect to see in there?" he went on. "Even by day, the dense trees shroud the light. 'Tis named Wychwood for good reason."

Abby snatched up her satchel. "Your words are great comfort, Edgar, but we must be moving on."

Jacob stood rooted.

As Edgar pointed into the forest, they noticed his finger shaking.

"Follow the path," he said. "Stray from it at your peril. Within one mile, you shall come upon the almoner's cottage. Godspeed."

"Why is the cottage set so deep in the forest?" Jacob asked, jittery.

"Wychwood grew around it, Mr Standish. The cottage is ancient - and haunted, some say."

"Pray begone, Edgar!" Abby laughed nervously. "I beg you."

Neither Abby nor Jacob had ever encountered a forest such as Wychwood.

They remembered the trees of St James's Park, and both knew the green spaces of Woolwich - Jacob through Standish Hall, Abby when staying with kin there before entering service - yet those places were nothing like this foreboding domain set before them.

They were city folk, accustomed to narrow streets, clustered buildings and throngs of people, stench in their noses and haste on their minds.

This was not that world - this tangle of claws born of the soil. It threatened witchery and dark ritual.

"What shall we do?" Jacob asked.

Abby frowned. Brave, he could be, in the face of earthly foes - yet this foe was said to be unearthly, and Jacob could not shake his superstitions. Even Abby, rooted in reason, found herself affected.

"Come," she said, handing him his satchel, "ere it grows yet darker."

Chapter Fourteen

Life & Death

S amuel never knew his elder sister, Paulina. She died when he was three months old. Two of the first four children were gone - the curse of a filthy, overcrowded city where disease thrived.

After Samuel's brother, Tom, arrived in 1634, their desperate parents sent both infant boys to a nurse, Goody Lawrence, in Kingsland north of the City. The air there was sweeter, and they hoped it would increase the boys' chances of surviving to adulthood. Samuel would later recall shooting his bow in those fields.

Grave circumstance plagued not only the children. Denied the privileges of a guild, John competed against established City tailors with limited success. His business struggled. With Margaret bearing and caring for so many children, they took in lodgers for extra income. These young men slept on truckle beds pulled out at night, crammed into the meagre floor space until the house at Salisbury Court resembled a cramped dormitory.

Bright-eyed and fleet of foot, little Samuel adapted to the chaos.

Outside, street vendors with carts announced their wares from Stocks Market and Fleet Market.

"Fair lemons and oranges!"

"Four for sixpence, mackerel!"

Apprentices opened shop shutters, swept shop fronts and traded gossip of the night before. The Fleet Street printers, arriving at their workshops before dawn, set type with mallets and pulled their presses, while hackney coaches delivered lawyers and clerks to Serjeants' Inn and Temple. Water carriers staggered among them with the day's supplies.

East stood Bridewell, once a palace, now a house of correction for the poor and dissolute, its thick doors muffling the cries from within. To the west lay Whitefriars, a ruined monastery turned liberty, where debt collectors and sheriffs held no power. So it became a refuge for debtors, coney-catchers and cutpurses, its taverns and brothels no place for the respectable.

This was London in all its guises, and young Samuel absorbed it all.

By age seven – amid stints with Goody Lawrence – he was helping Margaret with errands, gathering fuel, fetching produce. That same year, 1640, another sister was born, named Paulina after her dead sibling. The eldest, Mary, was gone, as was brother John, who died at age eight.

More children followed: Jacob, Robert, a second John – Jacob would not survive his first year – and Sarah, whose remaining days were few.

Of Samuel's ten siblings, seven perished in childhood.

Life crushed John and Margaret Pepys. St Bride's bell tolled so often for one of their own, while outside their walls England lurched from crisis to crisis.

For eleven years, King Charles had ruled without Parliament – tyranny, many called it – until summoning the Short Parliament in 1640 to raise money for his wars in Scotland. Bailiffs pounded on John's door, demanding coin beyond his means. All the children heard it; only the older ones understood.

Trouble brewed at St Bride's, too. Archbishop Laud's reforms stoked fears of a return to Catholicism. The Pepyses noticed the communion table had moved east, and new ornaments seemed gaudier – signs, said the whispers, of creeping popery.

Tension gripped the city.

Apprentices filled the streets, chanting, "No bishops! No popery!"

Meanwhile, the Member of Parliament for Cambridge, Oliver Cromwell, built a reputation for opposition, backed by Puritan reformers.

England slid toward civil war.

Chapter Fifteen

The Cottage

Edgar had been right. Wychwood's trees swallowed light.

Branches barred their way at every turn, and the path, such as it was, vanished at times. Twigs scratched, holly and bramble clawed at their clothes, nettles stung. They pushed through with flailing arms.

Fallen branches snapped underfoot, the sound carrying into the gloom. Dense trunks rose around them, offering no escape.

Jacob's feet grew leaden, and Abby found herself out front.

"Are we there yet?" he called, almost in a whimper.

"Not far," she lied, seeing only more forest ahead.

She had lost all sense of distance. One mile, Edgar had said. How long had they battled through Wychwood? It felt like an age.

Then she froze, peering through the trees.

"Jacob!" She beckoned him forward. "Quickly."

He joined her, breathing quickly.

"Look." She pointed ahead.

"A light! It must be the cottage!"

She clamped a hand over his mouth. *"Keep your voice down."*

He stared at her, confused.

"If the cottage is said to be abandoned," she hissed, "then who lit that lamp?"

Though they approached with stealth, every footfall cracked and echoed. Autumn had stripped the trees bare, and now each step betrayed them.

Jacob halted Abby. "Did Edgar prepare the cottage for our arrival?"

"The poor man was too terrified to set foot in here."

"Another of His Lordship's servants, perhaps?"

She chose not to reply.

The trees gave way to a clearing, and there stood the almoner's cottage, a relic of the nunnery, centuries old. Its walls were rough stone, darkened by lichen and damp, as if grown from the forest floor. The roof sagged beneath moss and creeping ivy, the gables crumbling.

A single chimney rose at a tilt. The windows were narrow slits, arched like chapel openings, covered with oiled parchment they had seen once before in Brampton, at the Grimston farmhouse.

Bramble and oak roots crept at the thresholds, as if nature would one day swallow the cottage whole. And still that dull glow spilled from one window.

They dropped to the ground.

Jacob straightened his periwig. "I should go."

She nodded.

"Will you follow?"

"Go!" she hissed.

The ground was strewn with decaying leaves in hues of gold and brown. Spying a fallen branch, Jacob weighed it in his hand.

It would have to do.

The door groaned like an old man woken too early.

Jacob froze, listening. All he caught was Abby's shallow breathing.

He flung himself inside, makeshift club raised, crying out.

Then silence.

Abby stood behind him in the doorway, not daring to enter. "Jacob?"

He appeared before her, making her jump.

"Empty," he said.

The almoner's cottage was a single room, its beams warped and furred with cobwebs. The floor was packed earth, scattered with sodden rushes. In the centre stood a wooden table beside an overturned bench.

A shelf of earthen pots clung to one wall, and in a corner sat a low pallet of damp straw. A guttering oil lamp stood in the middle window.

Abby broke the silence. "Someone was here."

She pointed toward the fireplace at the far end. Soot-blackened, its flagstones polished by years of tread, a kettle hung above the ash and embers - still faintly smouldering.

The room should have reeked of mould, its surfaces dusted with frost. Yet this was no icy cave.

Jacob hastened to the hearth and placed a hand on the kettle. "Still warm."

"We should fetch our satchels," she said.

"What of the lamp? This fire?"

"No ghost seeks light and warmth, Jacob. We're safe. Whoever was here is gone. We scared them away."

Abby set about tidying the place, though there was little she could do to make it welcoming.

She threw out the straw from the pallet and laid out their thick woollen blankets. They would sleep beside one another against the cold - perhaps also the fear - with no one about to speak ill of them.

She lit a fire, brushed debris from the table, and set out bread and cheese on the wooden trencher she had packed. Then, eyeing the door, she scrubbed and worked the rusted bolt until it moved freely.

Both were parched. They settled on the bench, gratefully gulping small beer from leather flasks. For the first time since leaving Ravenscourt Manor, they felt able to smile.

They pondered the physician's lot, and who might wish him dead.

Since the witchcraft hearing and the discovery of his dalliance with the stablemaid, village whispers had turned against him. His casebook since showed fewer patients, which must have hurt his income. The emptied decanter suggested he had taken to drink.

He had scrawled "M tells me the old woman's fevered secrets. Dare I act?" among his notes. The words, they agreed, of a desperate, conflicted man.

Did he steal Mr Pepys's gold? Talk in The Bull deemed it possible - though the same gossips also blamed the Grimstons.

"We found broad pieces in his chest," Jacob pointed out.

"Four of them," she countered, "when Mr Pepys's hoard must number in the thousands."

"Then why hide them?"

She gave a tight grin. "To ensure they aren't stolen?"

He closed his eyes and shook his head.

"Did it strike you as odd," she added, "examining eyes at night, as Bramwell did with John and Margaret Pepys?"

He tore off some bread. "Perhaps."

"And on January fourth - when whispers of the gold began, and the night hunters besieged the garden."

Jacob set his jaw. "It seems unthinkable. Lord Fairfax's personal physician - a gold thief? I should sooner suspect that wretched servant."

"Edgar?" she spluttered.

"I dislike him. He lives on the Ravenscourt estate, close to Bramwell, and seemed mighty keen to put the fear of God into us. Do you believe this cottage is haunted?"

She did not scoff, as he had expected, but let her gaze drift around the room. He followed it.

Tightening, she raised a hand. "Hush!"

He drew his arms to his chest, glancing left and right. "What is it?"

"Do you not hear it?"

He reached for her hand, pawing blindly. "Hear what?"

She began tapping on the table.

Rat-a-tat-tat rat-a-tat-tat

Her cheeks pouted with suppressed merriment.

He straightened sharply. "Why would you...?"

"Jacob, I was merely playing. I thought..."

"You thought what?" His voice was strained.

She studied his face, seeing something she had not expected. "Forgive me. I didn't realise…"

He turned away, pulled off his periwig, and ran a hand through his close-cropped hair. "Nay, forgive me. But I have seen a ghost once before, and 'twas no laughing matter."

Chapter Sixteen

The Demon of Spreyton

"You've seen a ghost?" Abby asked. "Where? How did it appear?"

"'Twas the ghost of my father. He came to me one night."

A dream, no doubt, she thought. "Did he speak to you?"

He cocked his head, wondering if there was mockery in her tone. "My father's words are betwixt me and him."

She had no wish to rile him further. "And I respect that, Jacob."

He retook his seat beside her, yet wary.

"As is only right," he said, gaze fixed on hers.

"Indeed." She rose brightly. "I packed some of Mistress Pepys's delicious plum jam. Shall we partake?"

As the oil lamp sputtered and hissed, they scoured the room for spare fuel and were relieved to find a jug of whale oil among those on the shelf. A trickle at its lip suggested it had been used lately.

Fuel replenished, the healthy glow lifted their spirits, yet threw shadows about the walls that danced like a witch's imp.

When the room fell silent, they strained to catch any sound outside. Every murmur of the wind, every animal's cry, every *crack* or *snap* in the dark stilled their hearts a moment.

As night descended, despite the thick stone walls, the chill bit only harder.

The fireplace had grown cold, leaving them a choice: venture out for wood, or take to the bed for warmth.

Though Jacob offered to go, she caught his reluctance and could hardly blame him. If he went, he would need the lamp, leaving her in pitch darkness.

"'Twill be a bind to find dry wood out there," she said.

He made no show of protesting.

They sat stiffly, backs to a crumbling wall, on the musty pallet. Their rough woollen blanket was tucked beneath them and tugged up to their chins. Still they shivered.

When Jacob blew out the lamp, knowing their oil was limited, the night consumed them. He had been eager, for decorum's sake, to maintain a sliver of space between himself and Abby; once darkness closed in, he drew her close and hang the consequences.

Eyes wider than Pepys's broad pieces, they peered into the dark, but might have been sitting at the bottom of a well.

Abby spoke, if only to break the dreadful hush. "We should visit the Watsons."

"Aye," he replied, barely above a whisper. "Where shall we find them?"

"According to John Pepys, they live down in the valley, close by the river."

"We know not precisely where?"

Her silence confirmed it.

They sat awhile, aware of their arms touching.

"We should sleep," she said at last. "There are long days ahead."

"Hold." He exhaled the word. "Let us talk some more. Know you… Know you any ghostly tales?"

She shifted on the creaky pallet. "But Jacob, you…"

"Aye, I fear the spirit realm." He paused. "Yet you do not."

"Well…" It was not entirely true, and Wychwood was sorely testing her limits.

"If I can endure the darkest of tales in this grim place," he went on, "then perhaps I may cure myself of fear."

He heard her puff out her cheeks.

"Try me," he persisted. "I offer myself up to the test."

Feeling for his hand under the blanket, she began. "Remember the chill you felt crossing Nun's Bridge? You know 'tis said to be haunted?"

"Nay," he replied, his voice rather high. "But I am glad to discover it only now." He forced a laugh. "Pray tell me more."

They shifted onto their sides, facing one another, he rigid as the stone floor beneath them. Their eyes had grown accustomed to the dark, yet so thick was it, like pitch, she could scarcely make out the hollows of his eyes.

Her tale continued.

The Benedictine nunnery had stood for centuries, until King Henry VIII, denied the divorce he sought from Catherine of Aragon, broke with Rome. He declared himself Supreme Head of the Church of England and waged war on the Catholic Church.

When the nunnery was dissolved around 1540, the nuns fled Brampton - yet one never left the village. She was dead, returned to earth as a spirit, damned to wander for all eternity.

Several tales of the Nun's Bridge ghost endured. To some, she was the same spirit that haunted Ravenscourt Manor. "She's known on the estate as the White Lady," Abby said.

He tried to clear his throat, but it proved dry. "How do you know this?"

"I ask questions."

Others swore to have seen the ghost pacing the bridge, some with a man, others with a woman deemed to be the Prioress. "'Tis said she was with child, having lain with a monk upon the bridge that bears her name. The Prioress discovered it, and she was executed and secretly buried. Others say she drowned herself for shame in the Ouse."

He pushed himself up onto an elbow. "You credit these tales?"

"Folk see many strange sights. Not all may be explained."

"Then you do believe in ghosts?"

"Who's to say those who saw her aren't mistaken? The mind plays tricks."

"Then this White Lady…"

But she was not finished. "And folk lie for their own dark or mischievous ends, Jacob. Paulina Pepys is no witch, yet she was accused and might have hanged. Her accuser, as well we know, lied."

She sensed his nodding.

"Tell me another tale," he said.

She peered at the murky shape of his face. "One more, then we must sleep. You know of the Demon of Spreyton?"

A sudden gust whipped in through the narrow windows, clattering the shutters. The next they knew, they were clinging to one another.

Gradually, they loosened their grip.

"The wind," he said. "Not the Wychwood Drummer."

She laughed unconvincingly. "It startled me too."

"This demon…" Jacob caught himself. "This so-called Demon of Spreyton?"

Abby paused. "There was a servant lad in Spreyton in Devon, named Francis Fey. He claimed to have met his master's father in a field - yet the old man had been dead for years. The ghost, staff in hand, bade the boy tell his master that certain legacies remained unpaid: ten shillings here, another ten there, and twenty more to a sister in Totnes. All must be discharged, said the ghost, or he would allow him no peace."

Jacob's teeth were chattering. "The cold," he assured her.

She went on, "The boy carried word to his master, and the monies were duly sent. Yet the sister in Totnes would not take it, saying such coin came from the Devil himself. The next day, as Fey rode to Spreyton, the ghost was seen seated behind him on his horse. Clasping its arms about his waist, it flung him from the saddle.

"When the beast came home alone, 'tis said it bounded into the yard with an impossible leap. And so all swore the tale must be true."

"Arrant foolery!" Jacob exclaimed. "If there is truly a Demon of Spreyton, then 'tis that idle scoundrel, Fey. He kept the sister's coin and conjured the ghost to give his tale credence."

Abby pulled the blanket tight. "Hold me," she said. "'Tis fearful cold."

Hesitating but briefly, he curled an arm around her waist, heart quickened by his boldness and by her closeness.

What harm can it do, he thought, *in so desolate a place?*

The long day's trials had taken their toll, and soon they were asleep.

Not long after Brampton's church chimed the witching hour, a sinister sound rose from Wychwood, echoing through the shivering trees.

Rat-a-tat rat-a-tat rat-a-tat

It rattled for a minute or two, then ceased, leaving deathly silence.

Abby and Jacob slept clean through it.

Chapter Seventeen

Encounter

Neither Abby nor Jacob had heard one word in the Watsons's favour - they were Brampton's pariahs, and their retreat into Wychwood was said to have had base causes.

Alexander Watson stole a neighbour's calf, it was told, and fled the magistrate's justice. His wife, Sarah, a midwife, delivered a stillborn child, yet the mother swore she heard it cry, suggesting witchery. Or else, she had cursed a salve, all but sending a villager to his early grave.

Lately, the two sons, Ned and Jack, had been spied lugging hefty sacks from the Pepyses' garden under cover of night.

Not one of these tales had been proven.

It was time to pay the Watsons a visit.

They had slept well despite the discomfort. Jacob woke to find his nose pressed against Abby's neck, and in horror sprang from the bed, dragging the blankets with him. Roused by the sudden chill, Abby leapt up, disoriented.

It was a while before they gathered their thoughts.

They ate quickly - cold meats from Margaret Pepys's larder, eased down with small beer - and packed all bar their blankets, grimly aware they would sleep in the cottage again that night.

"Should we take our satchels?" Jacob asked.

"If someone was staying here and ran when we arrived, it may be wise."

"Who do you think they were? A vagrant?"

She picked up her satchel and weighed it. It was heavier than she remembered. "Or we might hide them outside?"

She made for the door, glancing back to ensure no possessions remained.

Hoisting his satchel over his shoulder, he followed. "At least the Drummer did not appear last night."

"Or we slept through it."

"I think not," he said, stepping ahead to open the door.

The sun was rising over the village, its light dimmed by Wychwood's myriad branches. Having hidden their satchels among ferns behind the cottage, both paused. The air was still, thick mist carpeting the forest floor, denser than any they had seen. When Jacob kicked out, it swirled about him, wisps brushing his face.

"Fie, this place has a life of its own," he said. "Which way?"

"South, to the river," she said, pointing.

The ground sloped gently that way, down into the valley.

He followed her finger. "But there is no pathway."

Abby scraped fallen leaves aside with her foot, gazing into the tangled forest ahead. "The forest grew over it, just as it did the almoner's cottage. We'll just have to push through."

"Then allow me," he said, setting off.

The going proved fraught. Thin roots tough as leather laced the ground, snagging their toes like trip-wires. Jacob, prone to toppling, was often sent sprawling, scraping muck from his palms. Prickly boughs barred their way, springing back as they pushed through, catching on their clothing.

It felt as if Wychwood itself sought to halt them.

Each footstep echoed about the forest - the only sound, as if no creature dared stir by day.

And the mist endured, like an army of ghosts.

Jacob railed and cursed, while Abby urged him on.

"How much further?" he demanded, his patience wearing thin.

Having no idea, she said nothing.

As the slope steepened, she paused, straining for sounds of the bubbling river. All she heard was Jacob's moaning.

They had been battling for an hour when he stopped, leaned against a thick trunk, and slid to the ground. Ahead lay a brushwood-strewn clearing, and beyond it piles of broken branches, haphazardly stacked.

"I surrender," he said. "Wychwood has won."

Abby dropped to her haunches before him, and silence fell.

She lifted her head, blinking rapidly. "Do you hear it?"

"There is nought here but…"

"Hush!" she snapped, finger to her lips. "Listen!"

But her hopes were wishful, mistaking the swirling breeze for the eddy of a river.

"'Tis hopeless," he said. "We should return to Brampton."

She glanced about. "How, Jacob? Which way would you go?"

With a snarl, he heaved himself to his feet and stumbled into the clearing.

A chorus of cracking branches split the air, the ground gave way beneath him, and he vanished as if swallowed whole.

"Jacob!" she cried, rushing forward.

He lay at the bottom of a pit the width of two graves and just as deep, broken branches scattered about him. He did not move.

"Jacob!" she cried again, more urgently.

With clenched jaw, he slid his hands back, pushed himself up and rolled over. He stared up at her, his face plastered in wet leaves and filth, his periwig, miraculously, holding fast. Spotting his hat behind him, he clapped it on his head.

"A trap," he said pointedly.

She gazed about. "We're close."

Jacob's unusual height proved an advantage, and he hauled himself out of the pit. He looked a sorry sight, as if he had wrestled a pig in its pen.

Abby stepped up to the tangled branches ahead and tugged at one. It held tight.

"This looks placed here by human hand," she said. "As if to halt our progress."

When no reply came, she turned to him. "What say you, Jacob?"

He stood frozen, staring over her shoulder.

"What is it?" she asked, sucking in a breath. "What have you seen?"

"A face," he hissed, ducking down, motioning for her to do the same. "A face among the trees."

On all fours, he joined her.

"A man or woman?" she asked.

"Woman."

"Then why such concern? Was she armed?"

"Nay… But so waxen, so like a…" He faltered.

"Like a spirit?"

He nodded, avoiding her gaze.

Before he could stop her, she rose, cupped her hands and called out, "Ho there!"

He tried pulling her back down, but she stood firm.

"Ho there!" She listened. Only the forest's swaying branches answered.

"We're lost!" she cried. "Can you help us?"

Then it struck her: Sarah Watson - for that was who she imagined the woman to be - was a midwife and healer. *I should appeal to her compassion.*

"My friend is hurt! He fell into a trap!"

Jacob, still cowering, began to protest. "But I…"

She silenced with an impatient hand.

"We need assistance!" she persisted. "I can't carry him!"

Only the breeze whispered in her ear.

Jacob tugged on her dress. "She will not answer you," he hissed.

Abby kicked him. "Get up, you great oaf. You're no use down there."

Reluctantly, he staggered to his feet, and together they stared into misty, God-forsaken Wychwood, where no sign of life stirred.

"What do you want?"

The voice, thin and wary, came from behind. Both started and swivelled in shock.

Before them - mere feet away - stood a woman. She wore a simple brown robe and cream apron, her red hair - as red as Abby's - tied back. So wan was her face, it seemed almost translucent, and her eyes were bright amber. A vivid bruise marred her left cheek.

"How did you come upon us so silently?" Jacob asked. "This forest gives away every step."

"What do you want?" the woman asked again, tight-lipped, appraising Jacob with a shake of the head. "I told him not to set that trap," she added quietly.

Abby gave a small bow. "I'm Abigail Harcourt. This is my friend, Jacob Standish." She had planned her words. "We serve Mr Samuel Pepys - you know of him?"

The woman's eyes narrowed, but she lowered her chin in assent.

Abby smiled. "We're here to clear your family's name, Sarah Watson."

"What know you of my family?" Sarah's lips curled down and her eyes flared.

"We're Mr Pepys's personal inquisitors; our names are known throughout London." She ignored Jacob's sidelong glance. "We once saved the King's life. Now we're here to help you."

Sarah took a step back, glancing about like a cornered animal. "We need no help."

"We're charged with retrieving Mr Pepys's gold, stolen from his father's garden. Your sons have been accused."

"Nay!" Sarah turned to run, but tripped and fell.

Abby took a pace forward with outstretched hand, but Sarah scrambled further away.

"We don't believe your sons would do such a thing," Abby said.

"They would not! They've not been to Brampton in months. We don't allow it."

Stretching out, Abby clasped Sarah's hand and hauled her to her feet. "Then let us help."

Chapter Eighteen

The Hovel

Abby had chosen her words with care - and lied when it suited her. She did not believe the Watson boys were innocent, yet neither did she brand them guilty, as others had.

She was an inquisitor, and she kept an open mind.

There were paths in Wychwood invisible to the untrained eye, masked by ferns or blocked by branches that shifted aside with ease, then fell back into place.

Sarah Watson moved with practised stealth, leading them ever downwards, her steps light as a wraith's. Several times, she turned to glare at Jacob as he grumbled, limping on his injured knee.

The river came into view at the foot of the valley, its low murmur soothing the forest's oppressive air, and then, glimpsed through trees, a wooden dwelling.

It was little more than a hovel: timber uprights, with handprints set into the daub, where it had been smoothed into place. The ragged thatched roof sagged, and two coarse-haired brown pigs rooted noisily within a wattled enclosure.

Firewood was stacked against one wall, sheltered beneath a canopy. Smoke drifted up through a hole in the thatch, for want of a chimney.

The clearing was hidden away, sheltered by the forest. The trees were older here, the trunks wider, the branches more gnarled, groping like talons in the half-light.

The place smelled of earth, damp and smoke.

"This," said Sarah, presenting the scene with outstretched palm, "is where we choose to live. Does it seem to you that we covet gold?"

Neither inquisitor spoke, but gazed about at the harshness.

"You say my sons stand accused of the theft?" Sarah continued. "The same young men who toil with their father, every hour God sends, making charcoal, raising pigs, to keep us alive? I think not."

A brace of partridge hung from a nail on the hovel wall - signs of poaching. Those were Lord Fairfax's birds.

Abby pretended not to notice. "May we look inside?"

"Nay," Sarah snapped. "You may not."

"Are your sons there? Ned and Jack?"

With the hint of a sneer, Sarah placed herself between inquisitors and door. "What business is that of yours? My boys and their father are away gathering wood. I showed you this place only to prove we are no thieves. And now I wish you gone."

Abby's glance flicked to the birds.

Sarah's eyes narrowed, and she edged backwards. "How would you feed your kin, if you were hounded from your home with false tales of witchcraft and worse?"

"We heard..." Jacob began.

"What you heard is lies! We ask for nought, but to be left in peace."

Jacob spotted something among dead leaves and stooped to retrieve it. It was a crude straw doll pinned into an old rag that passed for a robe.

Sarah snatched it from him and retreated to her door.

Abby and Jacob had seen similar dolls in Brampton - poppets, used for witchcraft.

"What is that?" Abby asked.

"'Tis... 'Tis mine," Sarah stammered, clutching the thing to her chest. "A childhood keepsake, and that is all." Her spirited demeanour was beginning to crumble before their eyes. "Begone, I beg you. If my husband catches you, he'll make you rue it." Her hand lifted to the bruise on her cheek.

A piercing two-note whistle sounded from deep in Wychwood, scaring birds from the trees with a chorus of clapping wings and squawking. Inside the hovel, something clattered to the floor.

Sarah's face froze in fear. "My husband," she gasped. "That's his whistle."

She hurled herself at them, bundling them down the slope toward the river. "Follow the river east, it will guide you from Wychwood."

Abby fought to stop. "But I have much yet…!"

"Go!" Sarah pleaded.

Chapter Nineteen

The Brothers Grimston

So desperate had Sarah Watson been that the inquisitors felt compelled to obey, even with so many questions unanswered. Dropping down to the river, shrouded in an eerie, static mist, they followed the overgrown bank back toward the village. The river rippled, and the forlorn call of a rook set their nerves on edge.

Jacob's knee began to throb from his fall, and he lagged as Abby pressed on.

"Hold," he called. "I need to rest."

She retraced her steps. He was sitting on a fallen tree, its flailing roots exposed, torn from the earth.

"I don't like it here," she said, perching beside him.

"Neither I," he said, gazing out over the river.

"This place…" She looked around. "It feels…"

"As if we are being watched."

She sucked on her teeth and nodded.

"Where to?" he asked.

"To the Pepyses'. I feel safe there." She wrapped her coat about her.

Wychwood began to thin, and after a half-hour's trudge they came upon a fallow field, a dirt track climbing northward, bounded by a low dry-stone wall. Their limbs ached and their minds were tiring.

Jacob looked back. "Must we sleep there again tonight?"

"Best not dwell on it," she said quietly, taking his hand. "Come."

As they continued up the slope, a thatched stone dwelling came into view. Both recognised it at once – how could they forget?

It was the rear of the Grimston farmhouse.

They ducked low, conferring in whispers.

"Dare we?" Jacob asked.

"We must confront them at some time. You saw them flee the Pepyses' two nights ago."

"Well." He rubbed his chin. "I saw three figures in the dark."

"You told me 'twas the Grimstons!"

He placed a hand over her mouth. "Hush! They may hear."

Gently, she removed it. "Jacob, we're inquisitors."

"Aye," he said, his tongue darting across his broken lips. "And sometimes I wish I were still a naval apprentice."

With that, he rose and hobbled toward the farmhouse.

"Hold for me," she hissed.

"Gladly," he said under his breath.

Jacob's rapping carried across the barren fields as they shuffled nervously at the bowed wooden door. No sound came from within.

He let his broad shoulders drop.

"Try the handle," Abby said.

He regarded her askance, then shrugged.

Finding it locked, he moved to a window and peered through the oiled fabric stretched across its frame. A single lamp burned inside. By its glow he could make out four tankards around a central table, but little else. He remembered his previous visit: the herbs hanging from the rafters, the piled blankets, the scent of bread.

How innocent the village could seem, while evil lurked unbidden.

"Hoi!" came the cry.

Then another voice, rougher still. "What d'you want?"

Then a third. "Who dares trouble the Grimstons?"

They were upon them in an instant, flushed of face and roughly whiskered, with hair like windblown straw.

They stopped as one before the inquisitors, hemming them in.

The tallest and oldest, chin jutting defiantly, smacked a filthy fist into his palm. "We heard you'd returned." He sniffed loudly. "Most unwise."

Jacob held his ground. "And who are you to bar our way?"

The tall fellow sneered. "Silas Grimston."

The stockier fellow at his shoulder spat into the dirt. "Elias," he grunted.

The shortest, barely older than Abby yet meanest of face, took a swig from a ceramic flagon. "And I am Jonas Grimston."

Silas shoved him, and he righted himself with a scolded look.

"I'll do the talking," Silas told him. Then he pushed Jacob in the chest, sending him backward against the door. "Did you not cause enough destruction when last you were here?"

Jacob stretched to his full height. "We are here on behalf of Mr Samuel Pepys, who is…"

Silas ripped off the inquisitor's hat and periwig, hurled them to the ground, and trod them into the dirt. As Jacob moved to pick them up, he found a hand gripping his throat.

Silas's face was in Jacob's, his breath reeking of rancid cider. "The same Samuel Pepys whose sister - Brampton's witch, and no mistake - escaped the noose on your word."

Abby caught him by the wrist, and he leered down at her.

"Your lady would defend you," Jonas said, shoving her to the ground. "How tender."

Jacob lunged, sending Silas reeling, but he was back in an instant, the two men grappling nose to nose.

Abby regained her feet. "We're here at Sir Edward Mallory's behest," she declared, and smiled as Silas turned to his brothers with a twitch of the eye.

Silas released Jacob, and his brothers slid behind him.

"The Senior Magistrate?" Elias said.

Silas turned and cuffed his brother's cheek. "All know who he is, clodpot."

"What'll we do, Silas?" Jonas asked, peering around his brother. "I wish these people dead."

Abby sidled next to Jacob. "Murder us," she said, "and you'll surely hang."

Jonas bared his ravaged teeth. "What of it?"

"Act wisely," Silas hissed.

"Aye, act wisely," Jacob echoed, eyeing Jonas, who bore no discernible neck.

Jonas broke from his brother's shadow, lunging at the inquisitors. Silas caught him and wrestled him to the ground.

"Begone!" Silas barked, jerking his head toward the inquisitors. "Ere I change my mind."

Elias joined the fray, tugging on his elder brother's shoulders. "But Silas…"

Abby and Jacob needed no second bidding.

As they fled, his injured leg forgotten, Silas called after them: "Don't think you've escaped, Abigail Harcourt and Jacob Standish – aye, I know your names. We Grimstons have plans for you yet."

Chapter Twenty

Jacob's Hunt

It was late afternoon when Abby and Jacob arrived back at the Pepyses' cottage. Their feet were sore, their hands and faces scratched and bruised, and they were spent. It had been the most trying of days.

They discovered their employer had been called back to London on naval duty, summoned by a messenger on horseback. He had left a note for them, which read simply:

I have all faith in you both. Do not fail me.

It did little to lift their spirits, weighed down by the prospect of returning to Wychwood for a second night.

Paulina was absent also, away with her suitor, Harry Packer, so Abby and Jacob settled at the table with John Pepys while his wife prepared supper.

Seeing Jacob wince as he rubbed his tender knee, John reached across and patted his arm. "Paulina will make you a healing salve when she returns."

Jacob glanced nervously at Abby. Paulina's salves were apt to start whispers.

"We encountered the Grimston brothers," she said. "They still believe Paulina to be a witch."

John chuckled. "As well they might. Sir Edward Mallory decreed otherwise, and his word is law in these parts - not those dreadful Grimstons. I heard one of them near drowned of late, rescuing his hat from the river." He slapped his thigh. "Enough talk of them. What of your hunt for my son's gold?"

On learning of the inquisitors' night in Wychwood, and their encounter with Sarah Watson, the old man laced his fingers together. His knuckles were knobbled and enlarged. "You're fortunate indeed," he said. "Alex Watson and his boys are rarely glimpsed in the village, save when selling their meagre wares, and she has not been seen in..." He stroked his chin, then seemed to forget himself.

"In how long, sir?" Jacob asked.

John's faltering memory reminded Abby of something he had told them previously. "You told us you made note of where you buried the gold?"

"I did?" Again, he thought for a while. "Aye, indeed I did! And I do believe I told my wife where I hid it - too well, for I cannot find it myself."

He called out to her in the adjoining kitchen, asking after the elusive clue.

The old woman appeared in the doorway, cradling a bowl and spoon. Seeing Abby and Jacob's hopeful faces, she bowed her head with a weary smile. "'Twas long ago, I fear. I remember nought of such a thing."

With that, she shuffled back to her cooking.

Abby pressed a hand to her eyes, concealing her frustration.

Jacob rose to his feet. "Fear not, Mr Pepys. I vowed I would find your note, even if it means turning this house upside-down."

Margaret reappeared in the doorway. "You will be careful?"

He began, it was agreed, in John's chamber.

"If that note is anywhere, 'tis likely there, among my possessions," the old man assured him.

Abby and Jacob had visited his chamber before - first door on the upstairs landing - while he lay sick with fever. Paulina had been there also, dressing his pillow with herbs, and the Pepyses' friend, Mabel Fenwick, who had tended the old couple while the inquisitors and Paulina were away in Huntingdon.

Abby was content to watch while Jacob went to work. For all his faults, his eye for detail was unsurpassed. If anyone could find John's note - if indeed one existed - it was Jacob.

Margaret had lit candles on the windowsills and writing desk, and the room's odour was of dust and tallow. The light outside was fading, and a draught through the rickety leaded windows made the bed-hangings sway as if alive.

Jacob stilled them with a hand, wary of ghostly presence, and was relieved when they stayed.

He cast an eye about the room.

The oak bedstead sat against the far wall, its mattress sagging under blankets. A chest lay at its foot, iron-bound and scarred, while the writing desk bore an ink-well and scattered loose notes. On the wall opposite the windows, a long shelf was lined with battered old tomes.

Starting at the papers on the desk, he found only household accounts. He hefted up the mattress, revealing a crumpled pair of breeches. Tossing them to the floor, he picked up a candle and dropped to all fours, shining it under the bed. Two pairs of shoes lay among the dust, and he tipped them up, hoping to find something secreted in the toes, as he had at Archibald Bramwell's.

Fortune did not favour him twice.

"Try the chest," Abby said softly from the doorway.

He turned the iron key protruding from its lock.

It yielded nothing but shirts and folded linens, stockings and a worn doublet, which he left piled on the floor.

John Pepys was no learned man, unlike his son, and a glance at the bookshelf suggested Samuel's hand at work, lending his father a pretence of scholarship.

Epistles by Seneca, Plutarch's *Moralia, Yearly Almanac 1659* by Vincent Wing, William Shakespeare's *Hamlet…*

With a blink, Jacob snatched down a calf-bound volume.

"What is it?" Abby asked, hurrying to his side.

He held the cover, its title glimmering in faded gilt: *Treatise on Coin and Bullion.*

"If he hid it anywhere…" Jacob trailed off.

He carried it to the desk and thumbed through the thick pages. Abby stared, restlessly clicking her fingers.

"Nought," he concluded with a sigh, slapping the cover shut.

"Here," she said, pushing in front of him. "Let me."

He snorted. "If I am unable to…"

He broke off.

Trapped in the crease between the cover and the frontispiece was a small piece of paper.

"You were too hasty," she said, teasing it out.

In a spidery hand were the words:

Mark the elder tree, there lies the key to health.

Squinting in the candlelight, Jacob read aloud: "'Mark the elder tree, there lies the key to wealth.'" A glint came into his eyes. "Then the gold is buried 'neath the elder tree!"

Abby shook her head. "Two problems, Jacob. There is no elder tree in the garden, only cherry trees. And the word is health, not wealth."

He snatched the note from her. "Show me it!"

When he saw she was right, he angrily flicked the paper. "Then it must be coded. By health, Mr Pepys means wealth."

"Let's ask him." She called downstairs, "Mr Pepys, would you join us?"

John's laboured footsteps sounded on the stairs, until at length he appeared in the doorway. "Did you find it?"

Jacob beamed. "Indeed, sir."

Abby remained silent.

He dug her in the ribs, and she nudged back.

"Mr Pepys…" they both said at once.

Grimacing, he bade her speak.

Abby handed John the note. He peered close, pursing his lips, then moved to the window and the candle there. Still he struggled.

"It reads: 'Mark the elder tree,'" she said, "'there lies the key to health.'"

John lifted his head, stroked his cheeks pensively, and repeated the phrase. "Those are more my daughter's words than mine. She is the herbalist in this house."

"That is Paulina's hand?" Jacob asked.

John sighed. "If only I could read it, I would tell you. But alas…"

"What of Margaret?" Abby asked.

John gave a rueful laugh. "We're both old." He gazed out of the window. "Yet not as old as these lands."

He slumped on the bed. "Seeing us all here reminds me of the awful illness that befell me when last you were in Brampton. Such a sorry state I was in." He pointed at each inquisitor in turn. "You were here, and you. I recall your faces close to mine. And… Who else?"

"Your daughter," Abby offered.

"Aye indeed. Paulina." He paused, before raising a crooked finger. "And the physician's mother… What's her name? I should know, for…"

"The physician's mother?" Jacob cut in, eyes alight. "Mabel Fenwick?"

"That's it!" said John. "Mabel Fenwick. How very shrewd of you."

Abby could only gawp. "Your nursemaid and the physician - they're related?"

"In a village such as this, most everybody is, my dear. Uncles and aunts and so many cousins. Long winter nights," John said, chuckling to himself.

Jacob pressed his fingertips to his temples, head bowed. "The portrait in Bramwell's chamber! I felt it rang a bell, but paid it too little heed."

Abby clapped her hands in joy. "And the words in his casebook! 'M tells me the old woman's fevered secrets. Dare I act?' What if 'M' is Mabel or Mother, and the old woman is Margaret, who let slip the gold's whereabouts while in a delirium?"

Jacob nodded eagerly, staring at John. "Both Mr and Mrs Pepys were struck down by the same fever. You may have it, Abby."

John smiled. "The mind plays devilish tricks, and my wife is ever speaking in her sleep. Why, but a few nights ago, she sat bolt upright and declared, 'The key to that chest,'" he pointed to the same one Jacob had searched, "'is 'neath the pillow.' Then she fell back and began to snore. I'd lost it, you see, and lo, I found it where she said! I've left the thing in the lock ever since."

He glanced at his strewn attire. "As I see you've discovered."

Chapter Twenty-One

Fine Fortune

*B*y *the time Samuel turned ten in March 1643, only three younger brothers - Tom, Robert and John - and Paulina, just two years old, survived. Of them all, he caught the eye: keenest to learn, sharper of mind, more confident. His parents singled him out for the finest education.*

It would require all their connections.

Young Samuel was sent first to Huntingdon Grammar School, away from London's civil-war tensions, where Oliver Cromwell had once been educated. John's family were scattered about Cambridgeshire and neighbouring Huntingdonshire, and it was through his kin that Samuel's path was secured.

His most valuable asset was Paulina Pepys, who had died in 1638. She was Samuel's great-aunt and had married Sir Sidney Fairfax of Ravenscourt Manor. Her son, Henry Fairfax, would prove Samuel's most enduring patron, contributing to his education and mentoring him into naval service.

Via St Paul's School in London, built on land north of the great cathedral, Samuel moved up to Cambridge University, entering the halls of Magdalene College in March 1651 as a sizar. This offered him a free education in return for menial duties: preparing meals, waiting on tables, custodial work.

The students, modest in number, learned Latin, Greek, rhetoric, logic and natural philosophy, attending lectures and engaging in debates. Samuel quickly established himself as spirited, and was apt to fall foul of the puritanical regime. During his final year, the Registrar noted that "Pepys and Hind were solemnly admonished by myself and Mr Hill, for having been scandalously over-served with drink ye night before."

His fondness for a tipple would never desert him.

Come the Restoration of the monarchy, when Charles II was installed on the throne, Samuel Pepys was married to a French woman – Elizabeth St Michel, seven years his junior – and installed in the Navy Office as Clerk of the Acts. He was wealthy, supremely content, and adept at cultivating favour. For Samuel's fortunes were about to improve through another family connection.

His uncle, Robert, worked on the Ravenscourt estate for Henry Fairfax. When he died in 1661, he bequeathed his cottage and 74 acres of land to his brother, Samuel's father. Acting with John as joint executor, Samuel fought off various legal contests and installed his parents in Brampton, with younger sister Paulina to care for them. In the event of his father's death, the cottage and land were to pass to him.

He knew the place well, having stayed at the manor as Fairfax's guest, and revelled in its endless meadowland and its contrast with London. This idyllic country refuge, he would discover, came not without a price.

Chapter Twenty-Two

The Tall Mountains

As Abby and Jacob made their way past Rebecca Thacker's cottage, night was falling, bringing with it a familiar dread. Every sound from forest, field and hedgerow might mask a demon born, or a murderer lying in wait. The village lay silent, as if all folk were in hiding, wary of the moon's light.

Brampton had succumbed to darkness.

Paulina had not returned, and they took supper with John and Margaret. Their discourse soon drifted from their son's lost hoard - a topic they seemed weary of - into family gossip.

Neither elder Pepys held much affection for Harry Packer, Paulina's latest intended. Like the man he had replaced, he was prone to drunkenness, yet also boastful, loud and far too enamoured by the sound of his own voice. An irksome fellow, in short.

When Abby asked what Paulina saw in him, John Pepys suggested his daughter cared more for appearance than character – and Harry Packer was, he begrudgingly confirmed, handsome.

John wiped his nose with a crinkled handkerchief. "He arrived soon after the witchcraft troubles, claiming to be a gentleman traveller, and tells all who will listen the ribbon in his hair is from Venice. Our Paulina falls too readily for such unlikely tales."

Margaret, who rarely spoke unless spoken to, added in a soft, croaky voice, "He seemed uncommonly interested in our Sam's gold."

A handful of lights burned in Brampton's windows, yet none so welcoming as those in The Bull. Beside it, the towering church, wreathed in shadows, seemed more yoke than refuge.

With every step toward Wychwood, Abby and Jacob found their pace slowing. Its presence felt palpable.

"Shall we?" he asked, as they reached the inn.

The damaged state of The Bull had not deterred the locals, who were there in number, waving their tankards and sucking on their pipes. The burning tobacco masked the odours of the recent fire with something a little sweeter.

As they entered, a ripple of hush spread from front to back, as the drinkers ceased their chatter and stared. They recognised a few faces: Robert Rance, with his black coat, seated alone, and at the rear of the taproom, Paulina Pepys, facing a tall man with his back to them. A red bow was tied in his hair.

The silence was replaced by an ominous murmur, sending Barty Nettlewood bustling from behind his counter.

"Welcome! Welcome!" he blustered, eyeing a few of the moodier locals. "My most favoured patrons! Pray, enter. Do."

Yet there was an edge to his voice, betraying his disquiet.

Jacob felt Abby catch his arm. "All the tables are occupied," she told him *sotto voce*.

Barty, performing an ungainly pirouette, noticed the same. Wiping his hands on his stained apron, his eyes alighted on Rance.

"You," he said to the wizened fellow. "Move aside, would you? Take a seat with some of your friends, and make way for these weary travellers."

Rance paid him no heed.

Abby and Jacob stood behind the innkeeper, keen to avoid confrontation.

"Look," said Barty, pointing out a pair of wispy-haired men with arched backs. "The Woodcock brothers have stools to spare. Why would you not join them?"

Rance's sidelong gaze slid to Barty. "Since they stink of the privy, is why."

"But Robert…"

Rance rose slowly to his full height, which was barely taller than the innkeeper. His mouth was set in a sneer, his knuckles whitening. "I said…"

The inquisitors felt an arm around their shoulders, and turned to find Paulina's companion standing grinning between them.

"I do believe," said Harry Packer, stepping back and bowing low, "that we have not been introduced. Henry Packer - Harry, to my friends. Therefore you must call me Harry." He snatched Abby's hand and kissed it.

Jacob made to speak, but Packer raised a finger. "Nay, Mr Jacob Standish. All in good time shall I hear your sage counsel. For now, you must join me at my table, beside my delightful lady. I would so hate to disturb this," he thumbed his nose at Rance with a sly wink, "distinguished gentleman's quiet."

"Good," said Rance, sitting with a grunt.

Harry Packer was indeed a fine-looking fellow, with thick golden hair tied back, high cheekbones, and lips full as plums. His coat and breeches were of the finest cut, if a little frayed at the edges. As he led them to his table, Jacob noted two small darned repairs at his back.

Paulina Pepys stood as they approached, gazing adoringly at her suitor. "Is he not the most genteel of gentlemen?" she said, flushed and beaming broadly.

It could not be ignored: the rather plain woman seemed alive in his presence.

"Sit, would you?" she added with uncommon confidence.

As they did so, Barty appeared with a jug of ale and an ingratiating smile.

"Nay, good sir," Packer said, shooing him away. "Ale will hardly suffice for such an occasion. Fetch your finest sack, I insist, that we shall make full merry." He slapped Jacob heartily on the back.

Abby caught her fellow inquisitor's eye and rolled hers heavenward.

He could only shrug apologetically, having rather taken to the fellow. Packer exuded a cordiality and deportment he had always aspired to, yet could never quite attain.

Packer leaned in conspiratorially, declining to speak until the others followed suit. "I hear you're here for the gold," he said behind a cupped hand. "A rum do, indeed. Are you poised like arrows, aimed at the heart of the culprit?"

"Indeed we are, sir," Jacob replied with undue eagerness. He felt Abby kick him under the table, and glared back. "Only this morning we discovered the physician, Bramwell, dead in his study." He savoured the gasps, and saw Paulina cover her face.

Packer stared aghast. "Murdered, Mr Standish?"

"Jacob," Abby cut in, just as Barty arrived with a tray of pewter goblets. "We mustn't speak out of turn. We know little, Mr Packer, is the truth."

Jacob thumped the table. "Bramwell knew of the gold through his mother and was likely involved in its theft. That he now lies dead implicates others in this foul plot."

Abby's cheeks burned. "All supposition, Jacob," she said through clenched teeth. "We bear no proof."

The innkeeper had frozen mid-pour. "Bramwell's dead?" he asked disbelievingly.

She nodded. "That much is true."

"Oh my!" exclaimed Barty, then announced to the taproom: "Archibald Bramwell is dead! Murdered in his bed!"

Uproar followed, as Abby shot Jacob a poisonous glance.

Sheepish, he turned away.

When calm was restored, Abby produced the note found in John Pepys's book and passed it to Paulina. Packer snatched it from her.

"'Mark the elder tree, there lies the key to health'?" He handed it back. "A clue to the gold's whereabouts?" His tone was a shade too thirsty.

"Is that your hand?" Abby asked Paulina.

The Pepys woman shook her head. "It looks like my father's, yet they seem my words. 'Tis true the elder promotes good health. The flowers, infused in water, cleanse the blood; the berries, boiled into syrup, fend off ague and winter ills. The bark…"

Packer patted her hand, as if soothing a child. "'Tis all most illuminating, my sweet, yet I do believe your brother's inquisitors are more eager to recover his gold, than to… cure a sneeze."

Fluttering her eyelashes, she lowered her head. "Anything you say, Harry."

Jacob tried to catch Abby's eye, but she avoided it. "Is there an elder tree in Brampton?" he asked.

"There are many, since the elder, as the note says, is key to health," Paulina replied, stroking Packer's hand across the table. "But the most venerable stands in the churchyard of St Mary Magdalene."

Jacob shot Abby a glance.

Her eyes widened. "Would the thief dare bury his ill-gotten gains in holy ground?"

The silence provided her answer.

Jacob shot to his feet, then Packer.

"Be seated," she snapped. "'Tis dark, and we must ask the parson's leave. We can't dig up a churchyard on words I still maintain concern health, not wealth."

"My father does make notes to himself," Paulina said. "We find them about the house."

Jacob retook his seat. "But we must try, surely? 'Twould be folly not to."

"Aye," said Abby. "We visit the parson at dawn."

As Packer sat, his eyes were glassy.

"Until then, we must return to…" Abby trailed off.

Jacob downed his goblet. "Aye, Wychwood. One more sack, perhaps?"

As if by divine intervention, Hatty Nettlewood appeared, bringing bowls of winter broth and a fresh jug. Though the inquisitors protested they had eaten, she would not hear it.

"You two saved this village from evil - pure evil, mark me - and I'll not forget it." Hatty nodded toward the door. "'Tis cold out there, fit to chill the bones, and a vengeful spirit abroad. You fill yourselves with my lovely broth. 'Twill do you good."

Anything, the inquisitors thought, to delay their return to Wychwood.

Packer nudged Jacob. "I noticed you admiring the ribbon in my hair, sir." Ignoring the inquisitor's blank look, he pressed on. "'Tis from fair Venice - a shade known as Venetian red. Aaah," he sighed dreamily, "how I long to return, and take with me my darling Paulina, that she also may know true wonderment."

He leant across the table and planted a kiss on the tip of her nose.

She giggled. "Oh, Harry."

Abby eyed him over the lip of her goblet. "You're a… gentleman traveller, we're told?"

He wagged a finger at her. "You've been asking questions."

She smiled, and he began fiddling with a gold ring on his finger.

"Aye," he continued, "'tis my burden in life to be ever compelled to discovery. The canals of Venice, the mountains of Austria, the…"

"Tell me about the canals," Abby cut in.

He drew back, allowing himself the briefest smirk. "Have you visited Venice?"

She snorted.

"Such a pity. The canals are… a marvel to behold. So broad. So graceful. So…"

She interrupted again. "And the mountains of Austria? So… tall?"

"Indeed, my dear." He smiled lasciviously. "So very, very tall."

Abby glanced at Paulina, who seemed lost in admiration.

"I fear," Packer added, "my powers of description do not match my urge to travel."

Abby raised an eyebrow. "Indeed not."

"What brought you to Brampton?" Jacob asked.

Packer sat back. "You inquisitors and your questions. Are they ever thus, my sweet?"

Paulina seemed not to hear, still gazing doe-eyed.

"'Tis our duty, sir," Jacob assured him.

"Indeed, indeed. I hail from Northamptonshire, Mr Standish, since you ask. My family are landowners, and my father most generous with his wealth. He affords me this life of, if you will, idle luxury. I remain forever in his debt."

"And Brampton?" Jacob pressed.

Packer's jaw clenched momentarily. "I have relatives in Huntingdon - Mary Bailey, my sister - with whom I reside. Yet, such is my wont, I craved to explore. 'Twas here in Brampton, as I strolled past Paulina's garden, I came upon this," he reached for her hand once again, and she gave it gladly, "vision of such beauty."

Abby distinctly remembered her employer, Mr Pepys, referring to his sister as "full of freckles and not handsome in the face" - a marked difference of opinion.

The night wore on. Hatty bustled back and forth, pressing fresh dishes upon them - salted meats, oysters, pickled fish - and refilling their vessels, until they were too pickled to refuse.

The discourse veered wildly, dominated by Packer's boasting, until folk began to drift away. When theirs was the sole occupied table, they had no choice but to take their leave. A fierce wind had begun to howl, made thunderous by the lack of a roof.

When it came time to settle the reckoning – a substantial sum – Packer rose gallantly and demanded to pay… then, with theatrical dismay, discovered he had forgotten his purse.

Paulina, heedless, obliged, saying her brother had that morning handed her twenty shillings, and refused the inquisitors' offer of recompense.

Chapter Twenty-Three

Windblown

"Where will you stay tonight?" Jacob asked Packer.

Gazing elsewhere, he reached for the door handle, missed, and toppled into the door.

Packer bellowed with laughter. "What a fine fellow you are, Mr Standish. I feel proud to call you a friend!"

Jacob blushed as Packer enveloped him in a gentlemanly embrace.

"And you're staying…?" Abby said.

Tersely, Packer released Jacob. "I reside, as I did inform you, in Huntingdon, Mistress Harcourt." Packer placed an arm around Paulina's waist, and she hiccupped. "Naturally, I would not sully my love's bed till we are wed."

Jacob found the handle and stood there holding it. "Yet Huntingdon is some way off."

"Not for a gentleman traveller such as myself. Why, I once walked from the Palace of Versailles to…"

Abby pushed past Jacob and flung open the door.

Three figures stood illuminated by the glow of her lantern, hunched against the wind.

Silas, Elias and Jonas Grimston.

"Well, look what the storm's blown in," Silas declared. "Little Sammy Pepys's precious inquisitors."

Jacob choked at hearing such shameful words.

"Have you been waiting here all night?" Abby asked mockingly, emboldened by the sack.

Silas clasped his brother's shoulder. "Elias here saw you enter…"

"That I did," Elias confirmed.

Silas scowled. "I told them already."

"Sorry, Silas."

"When I speak, you say nought."

"Sorry, Silas."

Abby and Jacob were already running.

But they were unsteady on their feet from the drink, and within moments had been bundled to the icy ground. When they were hauled up, Abby swore she caught a smile play on Harry Packer's lips as he slipped an arm around his bride-to-be.

Silas may have seen it, too, since he turned to Packer while the inquisitors struggled. "You, sir. What's your name?"

"'Tis Harry Packer," Elias blurted.

One hand gripping Abby's coat, Silas cuffed his brother with the other. "Fool! What did I tell you? You may know of him. I do not."

Packer bowed, bidding Paulina do the same. "I am indeed Harry Packer, sir. Gentleman traveller."

"Then be on your way, Mr Packer," Silas said. "The Grimstons have no quarrel with you."

Grabbing Paulina's hand, Packer pulled her towards her home, abandoning Abby and Jacob to the brothers' clutches.

It took two of them – Jonas and Elias – to hold Jacob firm, arms twisted behind his back, as he writhed and cursed.

Abby gave up battling Silas's brute strength. The Grimstons toiled in the fields, and the city folk were no match for them.

"What do you want with us?" she asked, defiant.

"Is it not obvious?" He spun her round to face him, eyes cold as winter, hair blown wild by the gale. "We want you dead."

Jacob kicked at him. "Your word means nought against ours. We have His Lordship's ear."

Silas shoved Abby aside, struck Jacob in the belly, and grabbed a handful of his shirt collar. "And we have Brampton's ear."

Abby threw herself at him. "Leave him be!" she shouted, tugging at his arm.

He turned, teeth flashing. "You leave our village by dawn on the morrow - or we'll build a gallows for you, *inquisitor*."

Chapter Twenty-Four

Headlong

Heads down, Abby and Jacob made it back to the almoner's cottage though blind luck and gumption. The gale snuffed Abby's lamp, yet also drove the clouds westward, revealing a glistening moon to light their way.

They threw themselves inside and sat silently on the floor in the dark. The shutters clattered and the wind shrieked down the flue. The room felt hollow, as if emptied by a death in the family.

Jacob was questioning his very calling as inquisitor. His life had been threatened, yet he had endured; the danger had fired him, offered a purpose he had never dreamed possible. He cherished the role, wore it as a badge of honour, and marvelled each dawn that he had not failed.

His brief time as an apprentice purser had ended in ignominy. His tutors at college had tired of his inability to learn. As the runt of the Standish litter, his parents had all but disowned him.

Yet here he was, growing, flourishing. His life had value. He had even - on rare occasions - found what he believed would forever be denied him: praise.

And Brampton... He had been here before. Then the village had been green; now it seemed dusted in malevolence. Too much talk of restless spirits and vengeance.

He pictured a gallows noose, pulled his coat about him, and began to rock back and forth.

Beside him, not close enough to catch any warmth, Abby only grew more determined.

Packer was a scoundrel - his very essence screamed it - and she would wrest Paulina from him. The Grimstons were farm-hand thugs, granted standing by long roots in the same soil, and needed taking down. How dare they threaten her life?

The physician lay dead, the gold was gone, the Watsons held secrets yet to reveal, and the village was sorely divided. Over it all loomed the spectral presence of the so-called Wychwood Drummer - yet to appear to her. Was he afraid?

Never would she flee Brampton. Not for all the spices in Asia.

Jacob sparked up the lamp, its paltry glow exposing his pallid, drawn features. "Shall I fetch our satchels from their hiding place?"

The wind seemed to be dying down, the resulting stillness no less unnerving.

She brushed a hand down his arm. "Nay, Jacob, let's sleep. There's much to do here. We must rest and regain our strength."

Once under the blankets, they shivered as one, too cold for slumber.

"You think we shall find the gold tomorrow, 'neath the elder?" Jacob asked.

He could feel Abby shake her head, whether in doubt or determination, he could not know.

"Somebody was hiding inside the Watsons's hovel," he added. "When the father whistled, we heard something fall. I would wager she shelters her sons."

Again, she kept her counsel.

He nudged her gently. "The bruise on the woman's face."

She ground her teeth. "Aye," she murmured. "The bruise."

"We should…"

Rat-a-tat

Both tensed, sucking in a breath.

"What was that?" Jacob hissed, though he knew full well.

rat-a-tat

"Quickly," she urged, throwing off the blankets, oblivious to the rush of frigid air.

rat-a-tat

Back-to-back in the clearing outside, they stood alert, hearts hammering.

"'Tis gone," Jacob whispered, his voice trembling with hope.

She tamped it down with a hand. "Listen!"

Rat-a-tat

"That way," she said, finger outstretched.

"Nay, there," he said, pointing the opposite way.

rat-a-tat

The nape of his neck felt pricked by a hundred pins. "Is it truly a ghost?"

But she was gone, off into the undergrowth.

"Come!" she hissed. "I need your light."

rat-a-tat

When they stopped, they clutched hands fiercely. The lamp's thin light picked out gnarled tree trunks, knotted and ancient, some resembling faces that mocked or groaned.

The Drummer sounded his tattoo in beats of three, then paused.

Their breaths shuddered.

Rat-a-tat

"'Tis closer," Abby hissed. "This way, quickly." And she was off.

"Hold for me!"

rat-a-tat

All Jacob could hear were their crunching footsteps and the voice in his head. It struck him as he stumbled on: he was chasing a spirit… Or, he reminded himself desperately, a man playing one.

He prayed it was the latter.

rat-a-tat

What if Abby is wrong, and the spirit is real? he wondered. *What would I do?*

He almost ran headlong into her.

She had halted, hand raised for silence.

"What shall we…?"

"Hush!"

But the only sound was their own rasping breaths.

The Wychwood Drummer had fallen silent for the night.

Chapter Twenty-Five

The Pearl Ring

Jacob woke before Abby and went outside to retrieve their satchels.

"Our food is gone!" he announced upon returning.

Abby shook herself awake, slumping as her surroundings grew clear. "Gone?"

"Stolen. By some pestilent knave!"

She sat up, rubbing her eyes. "But how? We hid it well."

"I can only assume we were watched."

She gazed about the fetid walls. "I feel it here also, Jacob. Wychwood has eyes."

He dropped their satchels to the floor, and she rose to join him, rifling through the contents.

It did not take long. "Aye," she said. "'Tis gone."

"You do not seem put out?"

She stood, brushing down the coat she had slept in. "Our bread and cold meats are gone; we weren't murdered in our beds." She sounded impatient. "We'll not starve to death."

They planned quickly, chilled more by the mood than the weather.

Besides unfinished business at the Watsons, they needed to dig for gold at the church's ancient elder tree. They were also eager to speak with Archibald Bramwell's lover, Alice Wilkins, who served as His Lordship's stablemaid. The two had been overheard whispering of gold in The Bull, and if he were involved in its theft, then likely she was too.

The Ravenscourt estate being closest, they resolved to seek out the stablemaid before racing to St Mary Magdalene. The church's distant bell had lately tolled the sixth hour, and time seemed in their favour.

The Watsons could wait. After all, they were going nowhere.

"How will we find their hovel," Jacob asked, "without the Watson woman as guide?"

"We'll have to travel via the river, as we did when we left."

Silence fell, while his mind ticked.

"The same path that leads past the Grimstons'?"

She hefted her satchel and made for the door.

Using the lace hem torn from her dress, Abby marked their path with ribbons tied in branches. It would spare them the panic of the night before. As she worked, she asked, "What did you make of the drumming? Did it not sound somehow strange?"

He gave a curt laugh. "Is a ghostly drummer not strange enough?"

She selected another ribbon from her belt. "Nay, Jacob, the timbre. It sounded… muffled, not sharp as I'd expected."

He considered briefly, but found nothing to say. In those racing moments of pure dread, timbre had been the last thing on his mind.

"Something," she tugged a bow tight, "troubles me about it."

As they emerged from Wychwood into the estate, it felt as though a cloud had been lifted. Both dropped their satchels and stretched their arms to the morning sky, drinking in the fresh aroma of the countryside. A deer grazing on the rise ahead pricked its ears, stared a moment, then bolted in graceful bounds.

Abby's heart leapt to see it.

The persistent mist had lifted, and the meadows lay swathed in frost that sparkled.

Jacob nodded to his fellow inquisitor, who returned a smile.

The omens felt good.

Passing through the orchards then skirting the manor house, they found the stables ahead, surrounded by fenced enclosures. No sign of life stirred, not even a grazing horse.

They found the animals in their stalls, stamping and whinnying, tossing their sleek heads from side to side. The smell was as ripe as they remembered, if no worse than London's streets.

"Alice?" Jacob called out.

It echoed bleakly.

Abby reached out to stroke one of His Lordship's fine beasts, and it backed away, eyes rolling.

They had met Alice Wilkins before, in this very stable. She was devoted to these horses – preferred them to the village folk, she had assured them.

At this early hour there should have been muck to rake and rumps to brush. So where was she?

The animals seemed to sense it, too: something was very wrong.

Hurrying back toward the manor house, Jacob turned a corner and knocked the oncoming Edgar clean off his feet. If the servant was irritated, he did not show it.

"Where are the stablemaid's quarters?" Jacob asked, offering Edgar a hand.

Edgar did not take it, but rose with dignity. "Allow me to show you," he said, striding off with a discernible limp.

Abby scowled at Jacob.

They passed the herb gardens behind Archibald Bramwell's apartment, through a courtyard wreathed in ivy, and reached a row of stone cottages bordering a fallow field.

One of the doors bore a horseshoe nailed above, prongs upward, believed to capture good fortune. The servant headed for it.

"Have you tried the stable?" he asked before knocking. "'Tis where she should be at this hour."

Both nodded.

Edgar rapped thrice, turned to Abby and Jacob, and nodded stiffly. They stood in silence until it was apparent that Alice Wilkins would not be answering.

"May we enter?" Abby asked.

That eyebrow arched.

"We…" Jacob began.

Edgar tried the door and found it unlocked. "His Lordship granted you the run of the estate, as Mr Pepys's inquisitors. I assume His Lordship meant these cottages also, kept at his favour." Jacob opened his mouth to speak. Edgar silenced him with a gesture, before adding, "I request only that you leave this place as you found it."

Jacob nodded soberly. "You may trust us."

Edgar looked him up and down, and left.

"What a curious fellow," said Jacob, heading inside.

If they half expected the scent of death, they were pleasantly surprised. The single-room dwelling was in disarray, the hearth cold, nobody present.

The only furniture was a three-legged stool. Alice Wilkins's possessions lay scattered in piles: soiled clothing here, straps and bridles there, papers and books, a collection of crudely carved horses, blankets… It looked as if the place had been ransacked, yet there was order within the disorder.

A scorched copper pot hung in the fireplace, and beside the hearth, stacked together, were a bowl, plate, knife and spoon. In one corner, two flagons stood with a cup inside a tankard.

Opposite was a bed of straw, as if Alice slept like her precious horses.

Abby eyed it. "When she lay with Bramwell, I assume 'twas in his bed."

The walls were bare, the rafters splintered, and the room smelled of the stables.

The search concluded quickly. There were no signs of blood, nor of any struggle, and the single clue, Jacob found.

In a wooden box on the mantle above the fire, he discovered a pair of silver earrings, a ring set with a pearl - and a Cromwellian broad piece.

"Just the one?" Abby asked. "Try the flue."

They knew from experience that secrets were readily hidden on the shelves within a chimney.

Jacob felt around the brickwork and brought down a shower of soot.

"Aye," he said, shaking his arm clean. "Just the one."

Chapter Twenty-Six

The Elder

"The broad pieces are identical," Jacob confirmed, adding Alice Wilkins's to Bramwell's three in his purse. "I feel certain they were complicit in the theft."

Abby opened the door to leave. "I advise caution. There is ever doubt in our game, Jacob."

It did not appease him. "Each coin is worth…" He stared at his fingers.

"Aye, twenty shillings. A fair sum, I confess." During her time as Pepys's maidservant she had earned a shilling a week. "Yet no great riches."

Jacob muttered something to himself.

"The question remains," she added, ignoring it. "Where is she? That she has vanished is mighty suspicious, with her lover dead and all the whispers of their talk of gold."

As they crossed Nun's Bridge into Brampton, both hitched up their collars. Earlier that morning, Abby had hidden her distinctive red hair beneath a large coif. Returning to the village placed them in mortal danger. Animosity festered, and the Grimstons were out for blood.

They ducked behind the hedges and stone walls bordering the roadway, glancing nervously down the valley to the Grimston land. Not a soul was about.

A baleful spell seemed cast about the place - the English village of witchery and ghosts - keeping folk indoors and even the birds mute. January was a time of repair and preparation for another long season ahead, yet this stillness felt unnatural: set in.

They slipped cautiously past the rear of The Bull and ran the remaining yards to the church. The graveyard and its ancient elder lay out of sight behind the vast grey-stone building, and they stopped at the arched door.

It would not do to dig consecrated ground without the parson's leave, they knew. They foresaw no quarrel, as emissaries of Mr Samuel Pepys.

Jacob seized the thick iron ring, lifted the catch, and the heavy oak door creaked open. With a furtive glance about, they stepped inside.

At one end rose the pulpit upon its dais; by the south door opposite stood a cracked stone font.

The walls were whitewashed, the rows of old pews plain. The tall windows, once filled with deep reds, blues and yellows, now held only patched panes of clear glass, the colourful saints long since destroyed by Cromwell's soldiers. Deep niches stood empty.

Even stripped of ornament after a century of up-heaval, the church exuded sanctity, its reverent silence in stark contrast to the world outside. Both drew a long breath of the musty air.

A door opened, and a hook-nosed, dark-haired man with a balding crown emerged, clad in a long black cassock. He seemed to float towards them in his dark leather shoes.

"All are welcome in the Lord's house," he said as he approached, voice soft as down.

The inquisitors shuffled.

Reaching them, he pressed his palms together. "Obadiah Larke, parson of this parish. Have you come to pay your respects?"

"To…?" Jacob asked.

Larke's cheek twitched. "Why, to the Lord, our Saviour."

Abby tightened a fist. "We're Abigail Harcourt and Jacob Standish - Mr Samuel Pepys's personal inquisi-tors. You know him?"

"Indeed. All Brampton knows the goodly Mr Pepys." He scratched at his nose. "I am less familiar with… *inquisitors?*"

"We investigate wrong-doing," said Jacob.

Larke took a step back, blue eyes bulging. "Wrong-doing? Is there…?"

Abby gave a nervy laugh. "Nay, sir, a small matter of our employer's missing coin. We were here in Brampton September last, though our paths did not cross. You may recall the terrible witch-hunt concerning Mr Pepys's sister, Paulina?"

Larke hastily crossed himself. "Speak not of witches, I beseech you. All manner of devils and demons seem lately to be abroad." He dropped to his knees and prayed, face upturned.

Abby and Jacob duly knelt, impatient for the "Amen".

When at length they rose together, she spoke. "We're here to beg your leave, sir. Our employer's gold… We believe it may lie buried 'neath the ancient elder in your yard?"

The parson cocked his head and cracked a wry smile. "Forgive me, but…"

It took a while to explain, but eventually Larke seemed satisfied with the strangers' tale (they having wisely left aside several of the grimmer details).

They filed out of the south door, Larke leading. "A fascinating tree, the elder. Many Christians hold that Judas Iscariot hanged himself from one," he said, closing the door behind them. "Others, that it wards off imps and demons."

They were in a bleak, uneven yard of grave mounds, mostly unmarked, others bearing skewed wooden crosses, all bound by a low stone wall. Flattened grass lay mouldering in clumps. The morning's frost lent the scene a pale, spectral cast.

"Then there are the medicinal virtues." Larke continued, stepping carefully past a recently dug grave. "'The young leaves and stalks boiled in fat broth doth mightily carry forth phlegm and choler,'" he quoted, and turned to Jacob. "Have you read Culpeper?"

The inquisitor had not, though he recalled the name from the tomes in the physician's study. He left the question hanging.

The ancient elder towered ahead, dominating the churchyard, bare of leaf and mighty of trunk, its branches dipping toward the earth as though in solemn repose.

"Well," Larke said, slapping the trunk, broad as half a dozen men. "Where will you begin?"

"We're too late," came Abby's voice from behind the tree.

When the two men joined her, they saw the wide hole at the elder's base, among thick roots. Beside it lay an abandoned spade.

Jacob bent down, scraping at the soil with his fingers. "Somebody left in haste."

Larke nodded. "That may be my doing. I heard a fellow loitering here, not long ere you both arrived. He fled as

I called out. I knew not that he was digging here, else I would have stopped him sooner."

"Did you know him?" Abby asked.

Larke rubbed his bald pate. "I saw only his back, and fleetingly. Although he did lose his hat as he ran, whence I glimpsed his hair which was yellow as corn."

Abby's lips narrowed. "Harry Packer."

Though Jacob dug fully around the base of the elder, he found only a shard of pottery and a Jacobean penny.

"I thought as much," said Abby, as he filled in the last hole. "The elder tree does indeed hold the key to health, as we've been told more than once. There's no wealth to be found here."

Larke crossed himself. "To seek treasure in God's acre is but to tempt the devil."

As they parted ways, the parson back to his church, Jacob let out a strangled yelp. "Sir, I near forgot to ask," he said. "You know the name William Rudd?"

Abby sighed exasperatedly. "Don't trouble Parson Larke with such things."

But he was eager for an answer.

Larke pondered briefly. "He numbers not among my flock. Should I know this man?"

"You know of the Wychwood Drummer?" Jacob asked.

"Jacob!" Abby snapped, like a mother out of patience.

Larke shook his head miserably. "All this talk of tormented spirits and…"

"You keep records of Brampton's deaths?" Jacob pressed.

"Aye," Larke replied, but wary now.

Jacob turned to Abby. "If we consult the death notices, and find no William Rudd, then we prove the Drummer is but a dire ruse."

She shrugged. There was some sense in his words.

Larke's expression hardened. "Nay, sir," he said, shaking his head vehemently. "You shall not sully this house of God with your heathen ways - prying into the very demons it seeks to deter. 'Tis a foul…"

"But sir…" Jacob tried to protest.

"Begone, both of you! You are no longer welcome here."

Larke turned on his heel, hastening to the sanctity of St Mary Magdalene, cassock billowing behind.

Abby shot Jacob a black look. "What did I tell you?"

Chapter Twenty-Seven

A Dream of the Past

Margaret Pepys dreamed fitfully one January morning in 1667, the furrows of her forehead deepening. In sleep her mind drifted back to the previous September, when Paulina and Rebecca had been damned with charges of witchcraft, and she herself had lain miserably ill.

In the dream she saw herself again, sprawled in fever on her bed, head pounding, belly churning, half-believing the plague had seized her. Sweat drenched her linen as she drifted between waking and delirium.

Out in Huntingdonshire they had escaped London's hell, but Samuel's tales of that ruined city haunted her, and she had wondered in her agonies whether a plague victim could feel worse.

Faces swam before her: Abigail, with those striking turquoise eyes; the lanky one, Jacob, who forever seemed one step behind.

"My inquisitors," Samuel had called them, which had almost made her laugh, even as she thrashed and burned.

Paulina had bristled at their presence since their arrival, feeling herself demeaned, thrust into the Brampton household like a nursemaid, when she so longed for one of her own.

Such thoughts mingled with bitter truths. John's tailoring trade had long teetered on the brink of ruin, ever a few unpaid bills from bankruptcy. When they had first come to Brampton, he held but forty-five pounds, most already spoken for in debts. How was a tailor, in his mid-sixties and ailing, expected to manage an estate?

So it had proved: the promised eighty pounds of yearly income had dwindled to twenty-nine after annuities and arrears. Once again Samuel had stepped in - fifty pounds yearly from his own pocket to keep them afloat. They had given him every chance - grammar school, university, connections - more than any other child.

Was it not only fair that he now repay the debt?

The dream twisted. In it, she jolted upright in her sickbed, clawing at the blanket. The chair beside her, empty when she had last closed her eyes, was now filled. An old woman leaned forward, peering. "How are you, my dear? Can I fetch something?"

It had taken Margaret's fevered mind a moment to place her: Mabel Fenwick, the physician's mother, meddler and gossip. "You were calling out," Mabel told her in the dream, patting her sweat-slick hand. "Something about gold?"

The awful woman had pestered her with questions. In her delirium, it had felt like an interrogation. As she continued to watch the scene as if from above, writhing and rambling on that bed, she heard herself say it. The fever had unlocked the deepest chambers of her mind, and she had remembered it – John's method for finding Samuel's hoard. And there she was, telling Mabel Fenwick.

With a start, Margaret woke in her January bed, heart pounding, the dream already fading. Before it vanished for good, she cast her racing mind back – and caught it.

Aye, she had it. She knew the key to finding the gold.

Chapter Twenty-Eight

The Anchor

"How could I know he would react with such ire?" Jacob protested. "It seemed unduly harsh for so innocent a request."

"He's a man of the cloth, for Heaven's sake. You can't ask to seek malevolent spirits in his parish records. 'Tis…"

"'Tis what?"

"'Tis what?"

Huffing, Abby stormed off.

She was heading - though neither had discussed the move - to the Pepys house.

"What is our plan?" he called out in frustration, running to catch up.

She turned sharply and pressed a finger to her lips.

When he reached her, she bundled him through a gap in the hedge bordering Rebecca Thacker's garden. The house had sat empty since Rebecca moved to Cambridge.

They crouched down, conferring in low voices.

"I wish to find Harry Packer, and trust he's with Paulina," she said. "He has much to answer for."

"He is not the only one with golden hair," Jacob pointed out. "What of the Grimstons?"

"'Twas Packer the parson spied digging for gold, I'd swear to it. He knew of the elder since you blurted it out in The Bull."

Jacob cleared his throat. "Yet… If he seeks the gold, then surely he cannot have stolen it?"

She gave a dry laugh. "He plays games, Jacob - with everybody."

"What of the Grimstons? They seem mighty keen to be rid of us."

"Aye, since they blame us for what befell their parents. They are high on our list of suspects, alongside Alice Wilkins… wherever she may be."

"The parson concerns me also."

Her mouth fell open.

He spread his hands. "The way he turned on us!"

"Turned on you, Jacob. For filling his church with tormented ghosts."

He straightened his periwig. "Then what of the Watsons? Masters of all Wychwood, who live in a hovel and can only dream of wealth. Their sons were seen that night bearing heavy sacks - and she conceals them from us. 'Tis curious, think you not?"

A conceited half-smile played on her lips.

It riled him. "I've worked alongside men like Harry Packer," he snapped, "and all are the same. Loud mouths, yet small breeches."

She spluttered. "What are you saying?"

"That Packer is a braggart, not a thief. He has not the stomach for it."

"We'll see," she said, rising.

They were surprised to find Margaret greeting them at the door, her usual reserve abandoned.

"It returned to me in a dream," she said in some agitation. "Come quickly."

Abby glanced at Jacob. "What returned to you, Mistress Pepys?"

"We know how to find the gold!"

"Not so loud, Margaret," came John's croaky voice from the hall.

John Pepys rose from his seat, using the chair-back for balance. "Up there," he said, pointing to the stairs. "I am but an old fool."

Abby rushed to his aid. "Not at all, Mr Pepys. But, pray, tell us… You've remembered your hiding place?"

He sighed wistfully, his kindly eyes resting on hers. "Not I. Margaret. We awaited your return, ere we dug. We've had visitors, you see."

"Bad folk," said Margaret, waiting at the foot of the stairs.

"The Grimstons?" Jacob asked.

John nodded. "And others - a mob. They seek you both. I sent them away, but they will return, sure as night follows day. There's evil in their hearts."

"Was Harry Packer among them?" Jacob asked.

John looked to his wife, who shook her head.

"He and Paulina are away in Huntingdon, at market," she said.

Abby grimaced and glanced at Jacob. He shrugged.

"Come," said Margaret, heading upstairs.

The four of them gathered in the old man's chamber, the bed, chest and desk all as before.

Margaret nodded toward the books on the shelf, one silvery eyebrow cocked.

"The books?" Jacob asked. "Indeed we found a note inside one."

She gave a derisive snort. "Concerning the health-promoting virtues of the elder? Only a fopdoodle would fall for that."

Jacob gazed at the dirt on his hands, wishing Mistress Pepys would return to her timid ways.

"Yet," Margaret added, "the book in which you found that note holds the key."

All eyes turned to the leather-bound tome: *Treatise on Gold and Bullion.*

"'Twas the anchor, if you will," John said.

Staring at the shelf, Jacob could only shake his head.

"Which titles lie to the right of *Treatise on Bullion?*" Margaret asked.

Abby read them aloud: "*Hamlet, Yearly Almanac 1659, Moralia* and *Epistles.*"

Jacob still appeared none the wiser.

Abby gasped. "I see it! Treatise - Hamlet - Yearly - Moralia - Epistles. T. H. Y. M. E. You hid your secret in the titles, Mr Pepys!" she exclaimed, turning to hug the old man.

He held his arms out stiffly as she did so, embarrassed. "Aye, then forgot it. Daft old fool."

Jacob tapped Abby on the shoulder. "Then Mr Pepys's gold lay buried in the herb garden, 'neath the thyme?"

She nodded, grinning.

"Is it possible it still lies there," he added, "undiscovered since the day 'twas buried?"

Chapter Twenty-Nine

Filthy Boots

Alas, it was not to be.

The earth beneath the bed of fragrant thyme was loose and easily turned, the perpetual frost having masked the darkness of the disturbed soil thereabouts. All Jacob found as he scraped about in the hole were two more Cromwellian broad pieces, dropped no doubt in haste.

He added them to the growing collection in his purse. "Six," he said, as the coins fell.

"Of thousands," John Pepys said, rubbing his unshaven cheeks. "And 'tis all my fault."

Abby bristled. "Listen!"

Voices approached.

Jacob darted to the boundary hedge and peered cautiously over. He was back in two long bounds. "They're coming," he said. "Many men, with arms."

"Quickly," John said. "Inside!"

Abby and Jacob lay cramped beneath John's bed, he so tall that his knees were bent to keep his feet from showing. She faced him, blinking, alert for every sound.

The first came as an unruly hammering on the door below, followed by footsteps and the creak as it opened. Immediately, an angry murmur filled the house.

"I told you already. They are not here." John's voice.

Next came Silas Grimston's – they recognised it at once, throaty and menacing. "Then you won't mind if we look for ourselves?"

A brief scuffle followed, then tense, muffled chatter.

Footsteps mounted the stairs, John's protests rising with them.

"How dare you invade my home, Silas Grimston! I demand that you leave!"

But the steps continued upwards, into John's chamber where the inquisitors lay hidden, scarcely daring to breathe.

Jacob saw that Abby's eyes were tight shut, and, beyond her, two great boots appeared, crusted with filth.

Jacob curled himself into a ball as John Pepys hobbled into the room, his brown leather shoes so much smaller than Grimston's.

"If you do not leave, I shall call for the constable."

Silas's snort near rattled the boards. "You'll find him downstairs, old man, among the other Brampton folk weary of your son's so-called inquisitors. Sorcerers, more like."

A roar of assent rose from those on the stairs, gathered to listen.

More steps sounded in the chamber. Jacob tilted his head and glimpsed the plain shoes and veined ankles of Margaret Pepys.

"Abigail and Jacob are no more sorcerers than you or I," she snapped.

Cries of "Pish!" and "Fie!" rang from the stairs.

Silas spoke. "What say you we test them - as we would test for witches?"

Margaret sighed testily. "They are no witches!"

But the mob was not for turning.

"Our gallows outside the village hall shall be our judgement!" Silas thundered.

"How dare you…!"

There came a slap and Margaret's yelp, then a loud thump that echoed through the chamber.

Folk gasped.

Abby opened her eyes, and the inquisitors saw Mistress Pepys sprawled on the floor, unmoving. She had to stop herself from crying out.

"Look what you've done!" John wailed, dropping to his knees beside his wife, patting her cheek. "Margaret! Margaret!"

The mood of the crowd shifted, uneasy now, even shameful.

"Leave them be, Silas," came a voice: Jonas Grimston's. "They're old."

"Aye, leave them be," echoed others.

"They aren't here, you base knave," John barked.

The heavy, filthy boots withdrew from the chamber.

"Accept my apology, sir," said Silas, all his menace spent. "I wish your wife a swift recovery."

After what felt like an age, the door downstairs closed and the clamour ceased.

Margaret opened one eye and winked at the crumpled inquisitors.

Jacob slapped Margaret on the back, and winced when she yelped. "Mistress Pepys, you were a marvel."

She smiled, perhaps for the first time since the inquisitors had known her. "Nought ever happens here," she said, shrugging, and made for the stairs. "Back to my kitchen, I suppose. What shall we have for dinner, John?"

They listened as her steps creaked away.

"You should leave," said John. "Silas Grimston won't remain cowed for long."

Jacob eyed Abby. "But where?"

"Wychwood," she said firmly. "The villagers steer clear, thanks to the Drummer."

He chewed his lower lip. "How do we make it there unseen? We dare not pass through the village."

John tugged his sleeve. "Head south and follow the river along the valley. Nobody works the nearby fields in winter. You should be safe."

Chapter Thirty

Lost

Margaret thrust a linen bundle at Abby as they left. "Take it. You'll not get far on an empty belly."

With a grateful nod, the inquisitor pushed it beneath her coat.

John offered a gentle "Godspeed", and they were gone, out into the meadow, Jacob ducking low as they made for the river.

The ground was hard and the air nipped at their faces. Dormant nature stretched as far as the eye could see, shimmering and innocent, yet beneath the surface that malevolent heart continued to beat.

Neither spoke, but glanced about fearfully, desperate to remain undiscovered.

The accusations of witchcraft had returned to Brampton, false as ever, born of suspicion and bent to devious ends.

And now the noose swung for them.

At the river they turned west, staying close to the water deep in the valley. They passed one man, fishing from the opposite bank, who drew in his net and slunk into the undergrowth the moment he saw them.

"Poacher," Jacob muttered.

Spotting a fallen tree, he dropped into its shelter. "May we stop? We have not eaten all day."

She hauled him up by the collar. "We stop when we reach Wychwood."

Picking their way over broken branches, they passed the Grimston house up on the rise and finally reached the forest's edge.

"Safe at last," said Jacob, then grunted at the irony.

"A little further," she urged, beckoning from ahead.

"But we are…"

"When we are safely in the trees, then we may rest. Until then…"

He had rarely seen her so driven. "Why such haste, Abby?"

She stopped and turned. "'Tis women they hang for witchcraft, Jacob. Rarely men."

One part of Wychwood looked much like another: a mass of trunks and a tangle of branches, stretching away into arboreal dusk.

As the panic of their flight faded, it struck them they had little chance of finding the Watsons' hovel, which they knew lay close by, let alone their own cottage, perhaps a mile away.

Neither voiced their fear.

Instead, they pressed onward through ever denser bracken, stumbling and cursing, longing for the journey's end. Wychwood only closed in.

Each step created a cacophony, and when they stopped: silence. Not a sound. Eerie as night, and laden with threat.

Overhead, through the skeletal veil of boughs, the light was fading fast. Neither Abby nor Jacob had remembered to bring a lamp.

"We're lost," Abby said at last, sinking to the earth in a small clearing.

Jacob slumped next to her, puffing wearily.

She pulled off her coif and ran her fingers through her hair. "What'll we do, Jacob? How will we escape this place? Which way lies the river? Where's our cottage?"

He reached an arm around her, and she buried her head in her hands. "We might die here."

"Come now," he said. "All is not lost."

She faced him, tears of frustration welling. "Is it not? Then guide us out of this God-forsaken place, Jacob Standish."

His hand shot up, face upturned.

"What is it?" she gasped.

He clamped a hand over her mouth, whispering, "I heard a twig snap."

"An animal?"

He shook his head, gazing about. "Who goes there?"

Another *snap* sounded, somewhere ahead.

She wrapped an arm around him for comfort.

Then she saw it – a small white face, dark hair, staring – and her heart leapt.

As it sank back, she let out a shuddering sigh of relief.

A little girl. Merely a child. No more than six years old.

A mass of bracken lay between her and the inquisitors, some as tall as Jacob.

"What's your name?" Abby asked softly. "Are you lost?"

The girl shook her head.

When Jacob began wading into the foliage, she backed away, big sapphire eyes round with fear.

Abby tugged him back. "Hold."

Reaching inside her coat, she pulled out Mistress Pepys's bundle and unwrapped it. Inside lay a half-loaf of bread, some cheese and slices of cold venison. "Would you like some?" she asked, displaying the tempting fare.

The girl's tongue-tip flickered out and she glanced about warily.

Abby took a step forward. "May we join you?"

Again, the child backed away.

"We won't hurt you," Abby persisted. "I'm Abigail. This is my friend, Jacob. We're lost, too."

"I'm not lost," the girl said firmly.

"Then perhaps you can help us," said Jacob, "We…"

"Hush," Abby whispered, edging a little closer and staying him with a hand. "Do you like cheese?"

The girl wrinkled her tiny, upturned nose. "What's cheese?"

Abby glanced back at Jacob.

"Try some," she urged, pressing onward. "You'll like it."

The little girl did not flee as Abby broke through the undergrowth. Her face was streaked with mud, her hair wild and unkempt. She wore a coarse shift and ragged gown, patched in a dozen places. Her feet were bare and ingrained with dirt.

Abby dropped slowly to her haunches, proffering Margaret's bundle. The child's eyes fixed on it, yet she stayed rooted a safe distance away.

"Take it," Abby coaxed, picking out the cheese. "You look hungry."

The girl's gaze shifted from the food to Abby, studying her.

The inquisitor smiled.

An arm shot out, snatching the cheese, and the girl backed away, sniffing at the hard yellow lump.

"Try it," said Abby, nodding eagerly.

The girl took a nibble, chewing tentatively. Her face broke into a broad grin, and she tore off a chunk. "Bread," she barked through the mouthful, thrusting out a small, grimy hand.

A hand on Abby's shoulder signalled Jacob's arrival. The girl stared up at him glassily, shovelling food into her mouth as if she had not eaten in days.

"What's your name?" Abby asked.

"Lency!" came the anguished cry, followed by an on-rush of snapping twigs and rustling dead leaves.

The child flung the bread and cheese at Abby, dropped to the dirt and curled up.

"Lency!"

The inquisitors followed the cry and saw Sarah Watson hurtling towards them, whipping branches aside, horror etched on her face.

Chapter Thirty-One

The Dainty Lady

The frenzied woman swooped in, scooped up the child and clutched her to her chest, staring wild-eyed from one inquisitor to the other. The little girl began to sob.

"What's your game?" she hissed. "Who are you?"

Abby held out her hands. "You know who we are – Mr Samuel Pepys's inquisitors. We're on your side."

Sarah sneered. She wore the same robe and apron as when last they met, now filthier. "I've learned to trust no one. Forked tongues, the lot of you." She pressed the child's face to her bosom. "Hush, girl."

"We…" Jacob began.

"Enough duplicitous words," Sarah snapped, and began to retreat, never taking her eyes off the inquisitors. "I don't wish to see you again. Tell no one what you saw here, or I'll set my husband on you." An unhinged smile crept across her lips. "Then you'll be sorry."

"But we are lost," said Jacob.

She shrugged, still backing away.

"Your sons didn't steal Mr Pepys's gold," Abby blurted. "And I can prove it."

That stopped her. "How say you?"

"There were five sacks, each heavy with coin. I've held but a few broad pieces, and no man could carry more than a single sack in each hand."

She could almost hear Jacob's mind turning the numbers over.

He licked his lips. "'Twould take… three men?"

Abby patted him on the back. "Or fewer with a cart - but you'd never pull it through Wychwood. We can scarce make headway ourselves."

With the child's sobs subsided, Sarah lowered her to the ground and guided her behind her back, shielding her from sight as if she might be forgotten. "You'd swear to this? To a magistrate?"

Abby nodded. "We seek only justice."

The little girl peered around Sarah's waist, and Abby cast her a smile.

"We are lost," Jacob persisted. "Can you help us? Else I fear we shall die in this awful place."

The Watson woman gave a thin snort, gazing up and around. "She's served my family well enough."

Jacob squinted. "She?"

Sarah let out a cackle. "Wychwood is no man - far too cunning and shrewd for that. She speaks to me at night, in whispers and moans. All manner of tales, such as you'd never credit."

"Will you show us the way to the almoner's cottage?" Abby asked. "We're staying th…"

"I know where you're staying," she cut in, tapping her nose. "Plenty of things I know, that you don't."

The Watsons' hovel was barely a hundred yards away, yet so well concealed amid the forest that the inquisitors had failed to see it. Wychwood surely revelled in its secrets.

At the door, Sarah appraised them one more time. "You'd best come in," she said.

"Your husband…?" Abby asked.

"Tending a burn at his charcoal pit. You're safe - for the time being." With that, she pushed the child inside and followed, beckoning. "I'll not ask twice."

The hovel's interior was close and dingy, its daub walls cracked and flaking. With no flue, the air lay heavy with smoke. A dented pot hung in the hearth, and bundles of dried plants and herbs dangled from the low rafters.

The earth floor was strewn with rushes and bracken, and in one corner a heap of flattened straw served as a communal bed. Five stools ringed a wooden table, roughly hewn and crooked. The room smelled of damp, smoke, and of the forest itself.

So thick was the air, and so meagre the light, that Abby started when at last she noticed the two young men seated against the far wall, staring at her. The little girl had joined them and was preening a straw doll - the same doll Jacob had spied on their previous visit. The same doll Sarah had claimed as her own.

Abby stepped up to greet them.

One lad, the elder, only glared; the other smiled almost apologetically.

Abby introduced herself and Jacob, and asked their names.

"I'm Jack," said the younger, and glanced at his brother.

The elder called to his mother, "Why would you bring these outsiders into our home? What would Father say?"

Their little sister, nestled between them, continued playing with the doll.

Sarah was kneeling, stoking the fire. "These outsiders shall clear your name, Ned. And yours, Jack. They're friends." Her tone betrayed a lingering uncertainty.

Ned spat on the floor. "We have no friends - and need none. We are family."

The brothers bore a likeness: both with their mother's red hair, and the same high forehead. Yet Ned was wirier, a little taller, harder of feature. Their hazel eyes told their stories. Jack looked as if he might keep a pet dog; Ned, as if he might kick it.

"We know you didn't steal our employer's coin," said Abby. "We can…"

Ned rose, rolling his shoulders. "You can what?" He leered at her.

Jacob tensed.

"Stop it, Ned," said Sarah quietly, still tending her fire.

Ned stepped up to Abby, his chest at her head height. "Father would slay such folk and bury them deep in Wychwood, where they'd ne'er be found."

Jacob slid a hand between them, and Ned slapped his face. "You think you can best me, city boy? I'll slit her throat ere you have time to blink."

Unnoticed, he had drawn a pitted, rusting knife from his belt, and now pressed it to Abby's neck.

When she tried pushing it aside, he pressed only harder, the skin on her throat whitening. Had the blade been sharp, it would have drawn blood.

Sarah shot to her feet, hands wringing. "Stop it, Ned. This isn't what Father would wish. We need folk, and these are good people."

"Says who?" Ned spat, thrusting his face into Abby's. "This dainty little lady's done no hard day's graft in her life." Then sneering, he growled, "*Why would she help us?*"

Jacob was set to interject when Jack stepped among them, gripped his brother by the shoulders, and turned him until they were facing.

"I trust them, Ned," he said simply.

His brother blinked. "Soft oaf." But his grimy face softened. "You'd swear to it?"

Jack nodded.

"Since Father…"

"Come, Ned," Jack cut in, heading for the door. "The pigs need feeding."

"Forgive my son," Sarah said once the brothers were gone. "In their father's absence, my eldest bears the load. There are times he knows not how to carry it."

Abby took her hand with a smile. "I'm sure they're both good sons. It can't be easy."

The three sat at the table, Jacob dwarfing his small, rickety stool. The little girl continued to play silently in the shadows.

"I need to ask you…" said Abby, feeling for the pocket inside her coat. "You were once a midwife?"

She drew out a folded paper, spread it on the table, and slid it across. Sarah took it and raised an eyebrow.

Abby told of the page torn from Archibald Bramwell's casebook, and the broken words that remained. "I made a note of them," she said, gesturing to the paper.

son present,
of child,
at hand. Agreed

t have I done?

"I take it '...son present' must mean 'Watson present'?" she added. "Were you there, when this woman 'of child' gave birth?"

Sarah stared hard at the paper. Then she drew a breath through her nose and gave Abby a pitying look. "You know not the half of it."

Abby leaned across the table. "Then tell me, Sarah. What did Bramwell agree to? What caused him such anguish? What had he done?"

Sarah stared defiant, yet her fingers twitched. "There are secrets at the very heart of Brampton that must remain unspoken. You know not what you mess with. Leave it be, I tell you."

Jacob spoke. "They loathe us too."

Her fingers stilled. "Who do?"

"The villagers. They wish to see us hanged, and have built a gallows."

"'Tis why we hide in Wychwood." Abby added.

Sarah's face fell. She rubbed her cheeks, sighing deeply, and a tear welled in one eye. She seemed unable to speak.

"You know how it feels," Abby said softly, lips creasing in sympathy. "To be a pariah."

"And I would wish it on no other," Sarah barely whispered.

Jacob thumped the table. "Then we stand up to them. A mob cannot be allowed to rule."

Sarah eyed him, head bowed. "They shall take our lives."

Jacob cast a dismissive gaze about the room. "You prefer banishment in a place such as this."

Her head lifted, eyes like slits. "This is my home, dog."

"Aye. And not much of one."

Abby quickly intervened, gesturing to the child. "Your daughter, I take it?"

Sarah stiffened. "We speak not of her."

"Lency?" Abby pressed. "A lovely name. What is it short for?"

Lips tight, Sarah only stared.

"Silence," came the tiny voice from the far wall.

Abby turned to the girl. "'Tis a beautiful name." She looked back to Sarah. "Her hair is dark. Yours and your sons' is red."

Panic flashed in the Watson woman's eyes. "I had her after we moved to Wychwood. She's mine, I tell you."

Jacob shot Abby a look.

The door burst open, and Ned tumbled inside. "The villagers are coming with flaming torches! We must away at once!"

His brother followed, pacing to the fire and kicking at it with a bare foot.

Sarah stood, face drawn. "They'll not find us."

"Mother," Ned urged, clutching her arm. "They're already close."

The fire reduced to embers, Jack gathered up his sister and was gone.

"Come," hissed Ned, hurrying after him.

As the inquisitors rose, Jacob nodded toward the far corner and whispered in Abby's ear, "Did you spy the drum there?"

Chapter Thirty-Two

The Rising

As they emerged, they heard it: the savage glee of the approaching mob. And through the trees, not a hundred yards distant, the dance of flickering flames.

"This way," hissed Ned.

Jacob caught his arm. "We must make for the almoner's cottage. You know it?"

The lad sneered, exposing missing teeth. "I know all Wychwood, dolt, and I owe you nought. Find your own way."

"I'll take them," said Sarah, glancing anxiously about.

"Mother, let me," Jack cut in, cradling his sister in both arms. The little girl snuggled close, eyes wide with fear and wonder.

"Nay, Jack. You take care of Lency. I'll do it. Head for the encampment. I'll meet you there."

Having shared a glance, her sons melted into the forest.

Wychwood might have seemed an amorphous prison to the inquisitors, but not to Sarah Watson. Nimbly, and seemingly untroubled by the obstacles the forest threw at her, she led the way through places that looked impassable, yet opened before her.

The noise they made was fearful, yet such was their progress that the clamour of those pursuing soon receded to nothing.

What had taken Abby and Jacob hours, Sarah covered in little more than twenty minutes.

At the cottage, they gratefully drew breath.

"I must leave you," Sarah gasped. "None know you're here?"

Jacob thought for a moment. "I believe not. But that we would stay in Wychwood itself."

"Good." She crossed herself.

Abby caught her hand and squeezed. "Go safely, Sarah Watson. Look after that little girl."

"'Tis a weight I carry gladly," Sarah replied, pulled free, and was soon swallowed by the woods.

Abby folded her arms. "That's not her child."

"If not," Jacob said, "then whose?"

A distant thunderclap rolled in on a hastening breeze, and the air felt more alive.

"Inside," said Abby, as the first heavy drops began to fall. She held out an upturned palm. "With luck, this storm will send our persecutors scurrying home."

They shared out the remaining venison, cut into ragged chunks, Lency having wolfed down all Margaret Pepys's bread and cheese. Abby suggested they save some for the next day, just as Jacob swallowed the last of his.

"You saw the drum at the Watson house?" he asked. "Yet you trust the woman?"

"Aye, Jacob, I do."

"What of her sons?"

"They would have been young when the Watsons left for Wychwood. The drum may have been a plaything."

He picked up a lump of plaster that had found its way onto the table and threw it at the wall. "You trust too easily."

"And you think ill of too many."

He narrowed his eyes. "What is our plan for the morrow?"

"We can't remain here, skulking like criminals, if we're to make progress."

"Indeed, and I would not dream of it. I say we speak again with Parson Larke."

"A man of God, thieving coin? I think not."

"Then who?"

"Come," she said, rising. "Let's sleep. Tomorrow promises challenges."

He was woken by a scream.

Abby's scream, he realised, as his muddied mind cleared.

In the blackness he felt her sitting stiffly beside him. Reaching out, he found her arm, outstretched, pointing toward the fireplace.

"I-I couldn't sleep," she said, riven with fear. "And there, in the hearth's darkness, I saw…" She swallowed.

"Saw what?"

"A face. A terrible face appeared. Like a spirit rising from its grave."

He sprang from the bed, struck his ankle on the bench, cried out, and fell to the floor. Muttering, he crawled the rest of the way on hands and knees, groping blindly.

What little moonlight filtered through the shutters revealed nothing.

"There is nobody here," he said.

"But I saw him. His face, thin and ruddy, with a trailing silver beard. He looked… pitiful."

"'Tis dark. You dreamed it."

"I did not." Yet doubt clung to her words, like leeches to a limb.

As Jacob pushed himself upright, it came - the sound of drumming.

Rat-a-tat rat-a-tat rat-a-tat

"Hurry, Jacob, outside."

"Was the apparition you saw… the Wychwood Drummer?" he asked, but she was already gone.

They stood in the clearing, heads twisting back and forth, waiting for the drum to sound again. The sky was clouded, affording only pulses of moonlight, and the trees closed about them more sinister than ever. No beast cried, nor trod its paths.

Rat-a-tat

"That way!" gasped Abby, pointing deeper into Wych-wood.

rat-a-tat

A faint orange glow appeared in the distance, among the dark sentinels of the forest.

rat-a-tat

It was joined by another, then another. And then, lit from behind by the three flames, a dark shape appeared.

Rat-a-tat

The shape moved.

rat-a-tat

And again.

rat-a-tat

The shape took form.

The form of a cloaked figure with a drum at its waist, beating out a lonely tattoo.

Jacob dropped to his knees, fingers clawing at his lower lip. "Oh Lord have mercy on us," he moaned. "'Tis the Drummer himself, appeared before us."

Abby's hand snatched his collar, hauling him up. "Hurry!"

She all but dragged him the first few yards.

Rat-a-tat

Pressing on, they made for the light, framing the Wychwood Drummer in a ghostly orange haze.

rat-a-tat

Both stopped dead, agog.

rat-a-tat

The Drummer rose.

Floated off the ground.

Abby threw her hands to her face. Jacob fell again to his knees and prayed.

"It… it cannot be," she stammered.

Then, all at once, the lights blinked out, and where the ghost had been lay only darkness.

"What the…?" she gasped.

Chapter Thirty-Three

Discord

Returning to the almoner's cottage, they sat in silence on the bed, too shattered by what they had witnessed to light the lamp.

She heard him rub his bristled face. He had not shaved in days.

Jacob spoke first. "When we were last in The Bull, and you in the privy, a fellow told of a man - a parliamentarian - who had signed the death warrant of King Charles. His own daughter cursed him, and he died soon after." He paused to gather his thoughts. "At the funeral, his spirit was met by a coach driven by a headless man. The headless man was the King himself. And once the spirit entered the coach, it burst into flames."

She waited.

"If headless men can walk the earth," he said, "then a drummer rising in the air may be all too real."

"Have you learned nought?"

He tensed. "I know what I saw with my own eyes."

"Do you not wonder at the lights?"

"How so?"

"What ghost needs three lanterns at its back, that we may see it clearly?"

He shifted on the blanket. *"It rose in the air, Abigail!"*

"Aye." Her tone was resigned. "I saw it, too."

"'Twas the ghost of William Rudd, who was hanged for stealing a drum."

"How many times, Jacob?" She slapped her palms. "There are no ghosts. Only men seeking gain through deception."

"'Twas the Wychwood Drummer."

She shot to her feet. He could just make her out in the murk, her fists clenched in frustration.

"Are you afraid of ghosts, Jacob?"

"Why…" He surely was. "Nay, indeed not. I…"

"You fell to the ground - twice - babbling like a child."

Now he too was on his feet, but his fists were clenched in anger. "How dare you! How dare you besmirch my good character. I have confronted danger willingly, whenever I was called upon - at Whitehall, upon the frozen Thames, at…" He racked his mind for another.

She cut in: "Yet not in Wychwood."

He growled low. "You think yourself so high and mighty, Abigail Harcourt. So much more high-minded than I. Yet all know it - you are but a maidservant garbed in finery. And it does not become you."

She flung herself at him, fists pounding on his chest. "I earned my place, Jacob! Your father bought yours with favour."

He grasped for her wrists, meaning to restrain her, but his hand found something cold and metallic - the new brooch she wore at her throat.

He pushed her away and sat heavily, aiming for the bed. In the darkness, he fell short, crashed to the floor, and howled in pain.

As he righted himself, he heard her giggle.

"Oh, Jacob, what would I do without you?" she said, settling beside him.

She found his hand in the dark. It was achingly cold.

"You bought that brooch yourself?" he said quietly. "You swear it?"

"You still think Lucius Marwood paid for it? My actor-ly admirer."

His silence was answer enough.

"What if he did?"

His head lifted.

"Here." She unpinned the trinket and pressed it into his hand. "It means nought to me. You have it."

"Nay." He pushed it back. "'Tis yours, Abby. You must keep it."

Chapter Thirty-Four

Intruder

Jacob woke the next morning with a head like a hangover, though he had not drunk so much as a small beer since leaving the Pepyses'. He noticed Abby was not beside him, sniffed the air and sat up.

He could smell smoke, yet their hearth remained cold.

Abby burst in, near tears. "The Watsons' home!" she cried. "'Tis ablaze! We must leave at once, Jacob. I heard voices out there. They're coming for us again."

Outside, plumes of black smoke drifted overhead from the valley. From the same direction came hollers and shouts, and the barking of dogs, growing louder.

"To the estate," said Jacob, snatching Abby's hand and breaking into a trot.

Compelled to keep up, she stumbled. He hauled her upright.

"Be careful," he urged, and raced ahead.

He was glad of the lace ribbons she had tied in the trees, marking the true path. It spared him the need to think.

At times he pressed too far ahead and stopped to wait. Abby's face grew scarlet as she ran with hitched petticoats.

All the while, the dogs' distant pursuit echoed in their ears, driving them on.

At the edge of the forest, they paused for breath, the familiar meadowland sloping up toward unseen Ravenscourt Manor.

One by one, figures crested the rise, heading their way. Even in daylight some bore flaming torches; others, pitchforks and long pikes, relics of the old war.

"Trapped," said Jacob, dropping to the ground and pulling her with him.

He had never seen her more petrified.

"We must go back," he said.

"But the dogs?"

He licked his lips, tasting the danger. "We had best be quick."

As he ran, he ripped down Abby's ribbons - anything to throw off their pursuers.

Their flight was a blur. They seemed to reach the clearing before the cottage in moments, so tumbled were their minds.

The mob sounded ever closer, yet - they were heartened - not so near as to be seen.

"Now what?" she asked, stamping her feet.

He gestured at the cottage. "Inside!"

But when he made to move, she caught his arm. "What if they find us?"

He took her by the shoulders, stooping till his eyes met hers. The look alone steadied her, and she realised with sinking heart how wrong she had been to question his courage. She had not meant it - heat of the moment.

"You know Wychwood as well as I. The chance of them finding this cottage is," he paused, grimacing, "we must hope, remote."

Inside, the inquisitors cast about feverishly for a hiding place, though they knew full well there was none. The grotty old cottage was all but bare.

Jacob kicked the bench onto its side, stamped until a leg broke off, and wielded it like a cudgel. "This will give a fellow a headache," he said, grinning weakly.

She knew him well enough to know he was bluffing.

"Sit," he said, gesturing to the bed, then sat beside her.

All they could do was wait and hope, as the dogs' howls grew louder and individual voices became clear.

"Inquisitors? Inquisitors? Come out, come out, wherever you are!" cried one.

"Our fine noose awaits you!" jeered another.

Abby wrapped her arm around Jacob's broad midriff and laid her head against him. "We're going to die, aren't we?"

A curious scraping, stone on stone, made them both lift their heads.

When they followed the sound to the fireplace, a head appeared from beneath the floor.

The inquisitors leapt to their feet.

Abby gasped. "You! I saw you last night! I knew 'twas no dream!"

The intruder hauled himself up through the hole in the hearth, dragged the flagstone fully to one side, and sat there. His clothes were little more than rags, ripped and mudded. His skin was leathery, creased and marked with sores. He was gaunt with a long, wispy silver beard, and matted hair to match

He looked a terrible sight.

Before he could speak, Jacob flew at him, arms outstretched, fit to strangle. "You stole our food!" he roared as he went.

The old man cowered, edging backwards into the fireplace

"Stop, Jacob!" Abby yelled.

It shocked him to a halt.

"Did you hear that?" came the voice from outside. Too close for comfort.

"Aye, it came from over there," another answered.

"Bar the door," snapped the old man. "Hurry. Then follow me."

Jacob shoved the oak table against the door, hauled the broken bench on top, and clapped his hands clean with satisfaction.

When he turned back to the hearth, the old man and Abby were gone.

Chapter Thirty-Five

Croot

A ladder led down into a passageway lit only by the old man's lamp. It stretched off into shadows, the walls shored here and there with thick timbers. The tunnel was high enough for Abby and the old man, who was scarcely taller than she, to stand upright. Jacob had to stoop – he was accustomed to it.

"What is this place?" he asked, peering ahead.

The old man ignored him. "Close the hatch," he hissed. "There's a handle 'neath the flagstone. Pull it into place. Hurry!"

Jacob needed no ladder; his head naturally poked through the hatch. With a final glance at the cottage, assured the door remained unbreached, he ducked down and slid the flagstone shut.

"What is this place?" he asked again.

"Not now," said the old man. "They'll be upon us if we tarry. My name is Amos Croot. Now, follow me."

The inquisitors kept close to the glow of Croot's lamp, their noses suffused with the odours of earth and clay, and felt, for the first time that day, safe. After a short distance, they reached a fork in the tunnel, branching left and right.

"I've something you must see," said Croot, raising a finger.

"What is it?" Abby asked.

The old man winked. "You're inquisitors, are you not?"

He turned left.

After some hundred yards, the tunnel ended at a clay wall, against which was propped another short ladder.

"Here, take this," said Croot, handing Abby his lamp.

Setting the ladder firm, he placed one bare foot on the first rung and reached for a rusted iron handle above. Sliding it aside, a pale wash of light seeped into the tunnel.

"Come," he said, climbing. "And when you see it, pray hold your tongue. Myriad are your enemies, and who knows how close they lie."

The three of them were in a stone building, scarcely larger than a storage hut, gazing down at the lifeless Alice Wilkins. In death, all the steel had drained from her.

She sat slumped against a wall, leaning to one side, her ashen face resting on a decrepit oak chest. Her eyes were closed, and her long auburn hair spilled across the lid.

"When did you find her?" Abby asked quietly.

"Why, only last night – but she was cold, poor soul. You know her, I take it?"

Jacob bent beside the body, tracing his long fingers around her neck. "Strangled," he said. "As was Bramwell."

Abby turned to Croot. "What's going on here?"

The old man smiled benignly. "I was hoping you would tell me."

Jacob stood and faced him. "Who are you? What is your place here?"

"Once, I was the almoner, providing alms for the poor," said Croot, scratching dry mud from his fingertips. "You were lodging in my cottage. You know, these are the first words I've spoken to a living soul in," he paused, recollecting, "two-and-ten years. I'm glad to find my voice still serves me."

"How old are you, Mr Croot?" Abby asked.

"A hundred and two," he lied proudly.

Amos Croot had long served the Ravenscourt household as their almoner, a title carried forward from the old nunnery days. When his zeal grew tiresome and his age made him of little use, the family turned him out. Yet he never truly left, haunting the tunnels and outhouses about the ruins, calling himself almoner still, a ghost of a world that had ended a century before.

The tunnels, he said, were dug of necessity in the time of Henry VIII, when the inhabitants of the nunnery feared for their lives. "They run for miles, linking the house with its outbuildings, that the order might flee to safety when soldiers came."

Abby gazed up into the cobwebbed eaves. "And what is this place?"

"The hermit house," said Croot, picking up a heavy Bible from the floor and blowing dust off it. "Brother Godric once dwelled here, in silent contemplation."

"You knew him?" Jacob asked.

"I'm not that old!" Croot spluttered. "Impudent young cur."

An involuntary glance at the stablemaid's still form reminded Abby of their purpose. "Have you heard the Drummer?" she asked.

"Ah! Indeed. 'Tis why I came here late last night and found this poor wretch. Alas, I was too late to save her." He traced a cross over his chest. "You hear him also, no doubt? I am slow in pursuit, ever one step behind. He beats his tattoo at times in the tunnels themselves. I…"

"'Tis why the drum sounded muffled, Jacob!" Abby cut in.

"I've something else to show you," Croot went on. "You heard the Drummer again last night?"

"We did," said Abby. "And saw him for the first time, clad in black."

Jacob clenched the old man's upper arm. "The spirit - it… it rose in the air," he said, paling.

Croot only smiled. "Did it now? 'Twould explain what I am about to show you."

The door to the hermit house was padlocked on the inside. Croot produced a thick pin from his belt, pushed it into the lock and twisted. The padlock fell open.

"A useful trick, given my lot," Croot said, pushing open the door.

Before them, amid the clutter of the forest, one tree stood out. Its lowest branch, thick as another's trunk, jutted straight out a dozen feet above the ground.

"Here." The old man scraped at the leaves among its roots, picking out a pulley with one hand and a coiled rope with the other. "Our spirit requires earthly means to rise."

Jacob raised his hands to his head and let out a long groan. "I am such a clot."

Abby reached out a consoling hand. "I did tell you," she said softly, then turned to Croot. "The Wychwood Drummer has an accomplice, it seems. And you know not who these men are?"

"I can tell you whom 'tis not."

Jacob raised his head.

"'Tis not the Watsons, for I have seen them at their hovel while the Drummer drums. Back in '60, however - when first they came to Wychwood - aye, then 'twas them, reviving the old myth. I saw them with my own eyes. They took it in turns, scaring folk away. Yet this Drummer of late, returned to the forest after so many years silent – his beat is different."

A loud crashing sound reached their ears, followed by a coarse chorus of cheers. All three glanced through the forest toward the place where the almoner's cottage lay.

"They've broken in," said Croot. "We must be quick."

Chapter Thirty-Six

A Choice

As Croot stepped into the hatch, Jacob lingered by the chest propping up Alice's body. He reached out to lift her head, then drew back with a shiver of the shoulders. "We should look inside the chest," he said.

"I already have," said Croot, halfway down the ladder. "'Tis empty. Yet…" He rummaged inside his threadbare coat and flourished a gold piece. "I found this beneath it, fallen through a hole in the base."

Jacob took the coin, studied it, and nodded. "Another broad piece from the time of Cromwell."

"They must have moved the rest," said Abby, "fearing we're on their tail."

As Jacob went to pocket the coin, Croot snapped his fingers and held out a hand. "Finders keepers, I believe?"

Reluctantly, the inquisitor returned it, muttering, "If only we were on the thieves' tail."

Abby paused at the top of the ladder. "We may know more than you think."

Jacob's brow furrowed. "Pray tell…?"

But she was gone.

Retracing their steps, the trio reached the fork in the tunnel. From a leather pouch at his waist, Croot drew out a stub of candle. "That way," he said, pointing ahead, "leads to another branch such as this. The tunnel on the right will return you to the village; the left, to the manor house, where you shall find yourself in His Lordship's library. Take no side-path - there are many, and some end only in darkness. Stray, and you face becoming lost forever."

He lit the candle from his own lamp and pressed it into Jacob's hand.

"You won't accompany us, Mr Croot?" Abby asked.

As the old man shuddered, smiling, she plucked a dead spider from his beard.

"Your battles are not mine," he said. "And even if they were, I am too old to wield a staff in anger. Yet there was a time…" His eyes misted. "Once, I recall, at the siege of Marston Moor…"

"We should move," said Jacob, tugging Abby's sleeve.

She resisted, held the old man by the wrist, and lightly kissed his cheek. He exhaled, and his eyes welled. One tear escaped, traced a meandering path down his cheek, and vanished into a crevice.

"Mercy," he said wistfully. "It has been a while."

"Where will you go?" Abby asked.

"Where will I not?" He grinned and took her hand. "The pleasure has been all mine, Abigail Harcourt."

"You know my name?"

He gave a small laugh and bowed his head. "I know much about you. I lay beside you both, on the floor one night, listening to your gentle breaths."

"The old man is touched," Jacob muttered to himself as they set off up the tunnel.

She heard it. "He saved our lives, Jacob."

"I might have fought them off."

"There are too many, you fool."

"Abigail, you call me fool once too often."

"Forgive me. 'Twas not meant that way."

He quickened his pace, causing her to hitch her petticoats higher.

As Croot had warned, side-passages opened left and right, reeking of the earth and disappearing into darkness. They heeded his advice and pressed on.

At the junction the old man had foretold, the inquisitors began to argue. Abby was set on taking the left tunnel, leading to Ravenscourt Manor and sanctuary, where no villager would dare tread without His Lordship's permission. Jacob insisted they go right: into the heart of Brampton.

"If we are to solve this puzzle, then we must be bold," he said. "The thief and Mr Pepys's gold lie in Brampton, I am certain of it. If the villagers take us, then we shall state our righteous cause and reason must prevail."

She sighed in exasperation. "They carry pitchforks and pikes, with no thought for true justice. They'll hang us."

"'Tis a risk I am prepared to take, in our duty to Mr Pepys. He would expect no less."

"Jacob, he wouldn't wish us dead!"

"I make for Brampton," he said, chin jutting, grim-faced. "Are you with me?"

"This is madness."

The candle flickered between them, picking out his gaze.

She knew he would not yield.

Chapter Thirty-Seven

Trapped

The tunnel ended, as the others had, in a clay wall with a ladder and handle overhead. Jacob was already straining at the iron handle when Abby caught up. The journey had given her time to think – too long – and her stomach had tightened.

If this was him proving his bravery, then she had unwittingly pushed him too far. It pained her – though not half as much as this rash decision would, if the Grimstons caught them.

"We can still go back," she said, her hand on his thigh, gazing up at the trapdoor.

He grunted. "This stone seems heavier than the others."

Inch by inch, he slid it across, yet no glimmer of light fell from above.

"What's up there?" she wondered aloud.

All she heard was Jacob's piteous moan as he pushed his head through the hatchway.

"What is it?" she hissed, pulse quickening.

Climbing through, he beckoned. "See for yourself."

When she joined him, she could not find the words.

The candle's dancing flame picked out four oak doors bound with iron, each bearing a small, barred window. The door leading outside bore no window at all.

They had been here before, locked in those cells, alongside Rebecca Thacker. Rebecca - Paulina Pepys's friend - had been jointly accused of witchcraft; the Brampton magistrate, Bulstrode Bennett, had ordered their incarceration.

"'Tis a nightmare relived," said Jacob.

Abby strode to the door and tugged at the handle. When it would not budge, she swung round to face him. "We turn back."

His jaw was set, but his eyes told a different tale.

She rattled the handle again. "We can't leave, Jacob! We're trapped."

Elbowing her aside, he tried the handle himself. When that failed, he barged the door.

"Well?" she said.

He pushed out his lower lip, unable to meet her gaze.

"We have no choice," she persisted.

Voices came from outside, and the inquisitors froze.

"God keep you, Mistress Hartwell!" A man's voice.

"And you, sir," came the reply.

"The parson," Jacob hissed.

"What of it?"

He banged on the door. "Mr Larke! Mr Larke!"

She grabbed his arms and they struggled. "'Tis you who trust him not, Jacob!"

He clenched his teeth. "Aye, and 'twas you who told us we have no choice. That we are trapped."

"We can go back!"

"Hello?" It was Larke's voice, from the other side of the door.

They froze again, arms intertwined.

There came a tentative knock. "Who's in there?"

"Jacob Standish, Mr Larke," Jacob said with raised voice, as Abby glared. "And Abigail Harcourt. We met…"

"Aye, Mr Standish, I remember it well." A pause, then he added, "Pray, what is your business in my lock-up?"

Heavy keys rattled, and a key turned.

When the door opened, admitting daylight and a refreshing breeze, Abby could not hide her relief. With rasping breath, she hurried through the doorway, narrowly avoiding the shocked parson.

Jacob followed, bowing lightly. "We are much obliged to you, sir."

Larke took a step back. "How in Heaven's name did you find yourselves in there?"

Having gathered her wits, Abby cast a glance up and down the lane. Mrs Hartwell was some way off, heading toward the village hall; the other way, at the rear of The Bull, Barty Nettlewood was busy loading crates into a cart. She thought about calling out to him, but stopped, wary of drawing attention to herself.

Across the road, St Mary Magdalene's loomed grey and mighty.

"We seek shelter," she told Larke urgently. "There are folk here who would see us hang."

The parson shook his head, perplexed. "Then we must be quick," he said, floating toward the church in his dark cassock. "Come, my children!"

Chapter Thirty-Eight

In Hiding

Obadiah Larke ushered the inquisitors into his vestry at the rear of the church, closing the door behind them. "You're safe here," he said.

Abby eyed Jacob. "We can't stay here forever."

"One quandary at a time, Abigail." Larke poured two cups of sack from a flagon on his desk. "Now you must tell me: Why in Heaven's name would the fine folk of Brampton wish to see you hang?" His vivid blue eyes bored into her. "I find it most untoward."

Something about his look made her shrink back, and she forced down the potent liquid.

The vestry was narrow and whitewashed, its flagstone floor worn and uneven. A narrow-slit window, set deep, admitted a pale shaft of light. A wooden cupboard had been built into one wall, its door fastened with a rusting lock. Beside the flagon on the desk, a great Bible lay closed. The dank odour of centuries past filled the room.

Even as they talked, they remained alert to approaching voices. Larke, however, grew dismissive of their concerns, as if they were exaggerated or even imagined, and Abby struggled to quell her rising frustration.

So she was glad when, after his fifth cup of sack - to their modest two - he rose and begged their leave. He had parish duties to attend to, he told them.

As Larke left, he pulled the wide ring of keys from his belt. "I think it best if I lock the door," he said. "Deter your pursuers from gaining entry."

"And stop us from leaving," Abby mouthed to Jacob.

She waited until the parson's footsteps receded into silence, then sprang to her feet. "You were right," she said sharply.

He straightened, looking briefly smug, then frowned. "Concerning what, precisely?"

"*The parson.*"

"That gentle soul? His voice is so soothing, I find myself drifting off whenever he speaks."

She shook her head. "'Tis a front. He hides something."

"How you change your tune. 'Twas I who first suspected him."

"And now I concur. I sense something which I cannot place, yet I trust my intuition."

He shrugged. "Then what does he conceal?"

She swept a strand of hair from her cheek. "What indeed?"

As he reached for the flagon, she slapped the desk. "I have it!"

He raised those overgrown eyebrows.

"Remember when we first met with Larke? You asked to see his parish records, concerning the death of William Rudd, the supposed Wychwood Drummer?"

"His mood shifted."

She widened one eye, nodding. "He told us, Begone!"

"Aye. He would not have us root for demons in his church. Those were his words."

Abby ran a tongue over her front teeth. "Was there perhaps another motive? Might there be something among those same parish records that he dearly wishes kept hidden?"

As one, they turned to the cupboard on the wall.

Jacob had picked a lock once before, in the undercroft at Banqueting House, using the pin from his belt buckle. Alas, this one stubbornly refused to open.

Frustrated, he struck at the clasp with the parson's flagon until it gave way with a splintering *crack*. The inquisitors stood stiffly, awaiting the onrush of footsteps.

None came.

Inside the cupboard, among the silver chalice and plate used for communions, liturgical books and parish valuables, lay a stout volume, as thick as Larke's Bible, calfskin-bound and speckled with grease, its pages lazily undulating.

Jacob pulled it out and opened it on the desk. Within, the entries inked in many different hands, of baptisms, marriages and burials, stretched back to the previous century.

"What do we seek?" he asked. "There are thousands here."

"Try April 1660 – the same month Bramwell tore from his casebook. Something of great import he wished forgotten happened then, concerning an illicit birth. What if it appears in the parish records?"

The relevant page was easily found – it being the only one marred by a wide ink blot, the black now turned to brown with age.

Jacob flipped the page back and forth. "If 'twas an accident, surely the pages either side would be marred by seepage also?"

He was right. Neither leaf showed any sign of staining, as if the words on that single sheet had been deliberately obscured.

The legible entries above and below the stain read: "2 April, 1660. Baptised: Thomas, son of William and Joan Catterick" and "28 April, 1660. Buried: Alice Hart, widow".

They compared the hand with the latest entries, and confirmed it was the same.

Obadiah Larke had written them.

Jacob drew back and whistled. "What does he seek to conceal?"

Abby pushed him aside. "While we have these records, there's something else I have in mind." She turned to Jacob. "How old would you say is Harry Packer?"

Some while later, the low creak of the church door opening stilled them both.

"Return it!" Abby hissed, pointing at the book. "Hurry."

"But the lock is broken."

She hunched her shoulders. "Just do it."

He had barely returned to his stool when Larke unlocked the vestry door and entered.

He found them at his desk, discoursing in hushed tones. Both avoided glancing at the cupboard, where the lock and clasp dangled by a single replaced nail, the wood about it splintered.

Larke bowed his head. "As I assured you: safe from harm."

Both forced a smile.

Did his eyes just dart to the cupboard? she wondered, tapping on the desk to gain his attention.

"What is it, Abigail?" he asked.

"I..."

The church door creaked again, accompanied by men's voices.

"Mercy!" the parson gasped. "They must have followed me here. You must hide."

Abby and Jacob glanced about, yet no hiding place presented itself.

"Quickly," Larke urged, ushering them across. "Behind the door."

They stood rigid, side by side, backs tight to the wall.

Larke was holding the door open when they heard Silas Grimston's gravelly voice.

"We seek Samuel Pepys's inquisitors, Obadiah Larke," he growled.

The parson stepped back into the room, allowing him in, gaze downcast and voice uncertain. "I have them here for you, Silas."

Chapter Thirty-Nine

Mock Assize

The inquisitors' hands were bound before them, and they were marched - hounded from behind - out of the church toward the village hall. The three Grimston brothers led the way, Larke beside them, glancing back.

The winds had stilled, the trees stood silent, and ash-grey clouds lent the afternoon a brooding air. It was the perfect weather to accompany a hanging, Jacob thought grimly.

As the lane branched - right, to the Pepyses' - they turned left and saw Magistrate Bennett's tall house, and opposite it the village hall. The same hall where the Witchfinder General's son, the unhinged Simon Hopkins, had held Paulina Pepys and her friend, Rebecca, captive. The hall where he had deprived them of sleep to wring a confession, and where Abby had pleaded the women's innocence before the Senior Magistrate of Huntingdon.

Now, as the ragged group approached, the tables had turned.

They were the ones on trial, just as the Grimstons had planned.

"You shall not get away with this, Silas Grimston," Jacob said boldly.

Silas turned and strode to him. "Save your breath for the hearing, witch."

Jacob glanced at Abby. "Witch? It cannot be."

A shove sent him sprawling to the ground, to the delighted cheers of his captors.

The village hall was familiar, save one detail: the gallows now erected outside.

Two thick posts with angled supports, and a wide crossbeam from which twin nooses dangled, their coiled knots promising a terrible death.

Abby let out a strangled gasp when she saw it, and silence befell the crowd.

This business would surely prove fatal.

The inquisitors were driven into the hall, footfalls and wheezing breaths echoing, as the Grimstons and the parson led the way to a tall chair set toward the rear.

The Senior Magistrate, Sir Edward Mallory, had occupied just such a seat the previous September.

It was not Silas Grimston who sat there on this occasion, but the parson himself. The three brothers stood on either side, Silas glaring, Jonas leering, Elias picking at a scab on the back of his hand.

The remainder - a dozen men, all unknown to the inquisitors, faces pock-marked and weathered - gathered around them, some defiant, others shifty, while two held them fast by the shoulders.

In desperation, Abby turned to the door, half-hoping it would be flung open by some daring rescuer. *Yet who might that be?* it occurred to her. Decrepit old John Pepys?

If she were to escape this dreadful strait, it would be by her own wits and guile. Even Jacob's strength was no match for such numbers.

"Begin the proceedings, Parson," Silas said airily, and was nudged by squat Jonas, who sniggered.

Larke reached inside his cassock and took a surreptitious swig from a leather flask. Those who noticed averted their gaze.

Silas kicked the back leg of his chair. "I told you to begin, Parson."

Larke turned. "I did not intend it should end thus."

Silas gave a hollow laugh. "Why so afraid? We're all friends here, are we not?"

A few among the onlookers nodded; encouraged, their neighbours mumbled assent.

"See?" said Silas, hoisting Larke to his feet by the scruff of his cassock. "Our judgement shall be just and our vengeance godly. And none shall breathe a word of this outside these four walls."

Jacob tried to step forward, but was forcibly restrained. "If your judgement were just, Grimston, you would not stage this... *mock assize* in secret. Rest assured, heathen – I shall tell."

Jonas snorted. "Your neck'll be so long..."

Silas cuffed him, and he cowered. "Silence, brother. Sharp-minded as you are..." He paused to allow the laughter to subside. "...'tis best I speak for we Grimstons. Since all here present are sworn to secrecy..."

He waited for the chorus of assent, but the mood was changing, the triumph of the march now replaced by niggling doubt.

"I said," he added, voice raised, "all here present are sworn to secrecy!"

A few mumbled "Aye", glancing about with tight mouths and shifty eyes.

"Say it, damn you, or there shall be hell to pay. *Aye!*"

A muted chorus rose.

"Again! Louder!"

"AYE!"

"Better. Now." He turned to Larke. "Parson, yours is the authority at this assize, and we..."

"That man is no magistrate!" Jacob cut in.

Silas clicked his fingers. "Silence him."

Abby watched in anguish as three men set upon Jacob, forcing an old cloth into his mouth, while the parson cringed in his seat. What could she do, bound and held, with so many men about? She would have to bide her time and avoid any futile move.

Jacob's protests reduced to a muffled, impotent rage, Silas looked to Larke. The parson, quailing, seemed to have lost all conviction.

"What are the charges?" Silas bellowed.

Heads dropped as those gathered found sudden interest in their feet.

"I ask again: What are the charges? You!" Silas pointed at an old fellow whose eyes were set oddly, one facing up, the other down. "Nicholas Marner. Did you not witness these two witches consort with their imps?"

Marner pulled off his hat. "Um. That I did, Silas."

Silas pointed to another. "And you, Christopher Arkwright, did you not see them lift your mare into the air, then snap its neck, so it fell dead to the ground?"

Arkwright, thin as a hoe and balanced on a crutch, nodded. When Abby glared at him, he turned away.

Dragging Larke from his seat, Silas walked him forward.

"We have heard these witnesses' dark tales of witchcraft, which seem incontrovertible." A smile cracked his face. "Now, Parson, pray, tell us your verdict."

Jacob writhed, protests muffled by the gag, and was pushed to his knees.

The parson blinked several times and began gnawing at his fingertips. "Guilty?" he said, tone riven with doubt.

Silas shook him. "Louder, Your Reverence."

"I wish for none of this," Larke muttered.

"Jonas!" Silas beckoned his brother. "Have a word with Parson Larke."

"Huh–huh," Jonas laughed. "'Twill be my pleasure, Silas."

Larke broke from Silas's grip, eyes bulging, hands raised in surrender. "Nay, nay! I'll speak. They are guilty."

"And the sentence…?" Silas tapped his foot, grinning. "We'll not make you watch, Parson, I swear it." He winked at his brothers, who stifled sniggers.

Larke frantically shook his head.

Sighing theatrically, Silas lunged, clasping a thick hand about the cowering fellow's throat. "I said," his face pressed into the parson's, "state your sentence."

"D-death," Larke gibbered. "The sentence is death."

Releasing his grip, as Larke darted aside, whimpering, Silas cast a triumphant smirk. "Good," he said. "Shall we repair outside?"

Chapter Forty

The Gallows

The wind had picked up, carrying one spectator's hat into a tree. Silas had stationed a guard at either end of the road leading to the village hall, ensuring no undesirable witnesses. This was no justice, as well he knew.

The inquisitors stood at the gallows, Abby's bound hands shaking. Jacob stared bitterly ahead.

How he wished they had never returned to Brampton. These village folk were more corrupt than any Londoner. In the city, there was a constable, beadle or soldier around every corner. Not here - not when they so badly needed one.

He felt his hat and periwig snatched from behind, and the chill on his scalp. He turned to glare at the fellow, who scampered away.

The noose brushed his hair, yet he could not bring himself to look up at it: the harsh instrument of his demise.

Instead, he glanced to his side, where Abby's hair whipped about her face in the ill wind. Her expression was steely, yet he knew her well, and caught the fear in her eyes.

"Stand!"

Silas's bark shook him from his introspection.

Two men had set stools at Abby and Jacob's feet. When he stood on it, the noose hung before him, all thick coils and frayed strands.

She followed, and the noose was lowered for her. She said nothing, but stared ahead.

The men before them glanced about, some fidgeting, others with clasped hands. All wanted this over with.

Silas gathered his brothers beside him, an arm around each of their shoulders, grinning as if they were three victorious warriors, not bitter, criminal farmhands bent on revenge. The parson was kneeling before them, head bowed in prayer.

Silas ripped the cloth from Jacob's mouth. Coughing, the inquisitor licked his dry lips. Then, to astonishment and jeers, he broke into sobs.

"Are you scared to face death, coward?" Silas taunted. "What say you?"

Jacob shuddered, sniffed, and composed himself, staring Grimston in the face. "I weep not for myself, knave, but for my friend." He motioned to Abby with his bound hands. "Our time in this pestilent place has been fraught with peril, and we have shared angry words, which I deeply regret. Abigail Harcourt has taught me so much in so little time that I can scarce believe it."

She gazed up at him, her eyes reddening.

He did not shift his gaze from Silas. "I offer my life in place of hers, since she deserves not this vile fate. There is only goodness in her heart. Spare her, I beseech you. Take me instead." He dropped from the stool to his knees, hands reaching out, imploring.

"Nay, Jacob," she said quietly. "I'll not have it."

"Silence!" Silas cried. "I shall speak."

A few in the crowd swallowed hard and shuffled uncomfortably. Still the parson prayed.

"Today, we avenge my parents," Silas said. "Whose lives were cut short at the hands of these so-called inquisitors, who abused their power and falsified evidence…"

"We did no such thing," Jacob interjected. "Our methods…"

"I said, Silence!" Silas raged, clenching his fists, madness in his eyes. "I tire of this waiting. Let us…"

"May I speak?" Abby said. "Will you allow me my last words?"

Silas rolled his shoulders, temper abated. He bowed mockingly. "Indeed." He paused, eyeing the spectators with a smirk. "*My lady.*"

Elias snorted in derision.

"Parson!" Abby said loudly.

Larke snapped from his supplication, but could not meet her eye.

"Parson," she said again. "Pray tell us what took place in April 1660 that was so bedevilled you blotted it from your parish records?"

Now he looked at her, blanching. "You saw?"

She nodded.

"I thought as much," he muttered, then seemed to gather strength. He rose to his feet. "I fear I cannot help you, mistress. 'Twas some trivial matter that now eludes me, unrelated to these grave charges of witchcraft. Shall we continue with the execution?"

A few murmured assent, and Silas nodded, folding his arms.

"Unhand me!" came the woman's cry, not far distant.

All heads turned. Those who recognised her recoiled in shock.

Sarah Watson punched her assailant square on the nose. As he fell back clawing at it, she broke into a trot.

"Come, Lency," she called to the little girl following her, straw doll in hand.

Terror overcame the parson, and he turned to flee.

Silas caught him and held him fast.

"Let us hear what she has to say," he hissed in Larke's ear. "Whispers have drifted about this village for too long."

Sarah stood before the Grimstons, Silas gripping the squirming parson.

"Sarah Watson," said Silas, raising an eyebrow, "who hides away in Wychwood, fearful of all company."

"No longer, Silas Grimston." She squeezed little Lency at her waist. "Nor shall my daughter."

The parson stopped struggling, and his hands began to shake.

Sarah nodded toward Abby and Jacob. "Set them free. They're innocent of whatever charges you've conjured – and you know it."

Abby called to her. "Parson Larke claims he knows nought of the events of April 1660."

Sarah gazed down at Lency, then pulled a torn piece of paper from her belt. "Perhaps I may remind him," she said, holding it aloft. "I ripped this from the physician Archibald Bramwell's casebook, the same night he wrote it. He was a conscientious man – some might say too honest – and tormented by it."

Silence fell as she read aloud. Even the trees seemed to listen.

"Though some of Bramwell's words remain in his case-book, I remember them well." She recited: "'Called in haste by Dotty N.'" Her gaze alighted on Larke. "'*Parson present.*'"

Murmurs rose as Larke buried his head in his hands.

Sarah went on: "'Parson present, much agitated.'" The murmurs swelled, and she paused for silence to return. "'At 12 delivered of child, though weak. Midwife Watson at hand. Agreed secrecy.'" Her hand holding the paper dropped. She glared at Larke. "Bramwell concludes his note: 'What have I done?'"

Even staring at a hangman's noose, the inquisitor in Abby did not desert her. Stamping her foot, she caught Jacob's attention. "Where the note read '-son present', we assumed it meant 'Watson present' - it didn't, Jacob. It read 'Parson present'. Lency's father."

Jacob smiled thinly.

"And this is the child?" someone called out.

Sarah tightened a protective arm across Lency's chest. "Fearing for her safety, I took her in as my own. Larke paid off her mother, and Bramwell too. In the parish register, he marked her as dead, hoping she would be forgotten, then lived in fear of being found out."

"He later blotted the entry from his records," Abby called across.

Sarah smiled grimly at her. "He's a coward who drowns himself in wine. I despise him."

"He must pay for his crimes," Silas growled, to a smattering of cheers.

Larke dropped to the ground, weeping. "Forgive me, Lord!" he wailed.

"The Lord may be gracious – but we shall not, *Parson*." Silas spat out the word.

Jonas tugged at his brother's sleeve. "Who is the girl's true mother?"

Sarah began backing away, pulling Lency with her. "I am her mother."

"She is not of your womb," a voice called from the crowd.

"I am her mother," Sarah persisted, still retreating.

The clamour only grew.

"Dotty N," said another. "Must be Dotty Nettlewood, Hatty's sister."

"Aye, I remember the young woman being with child."

"And then one day, not… Where did she go?"

"That girl must be returned to her rightful mother."

Sarah halted her retreat. "Her mother abandoned her!"

"It matters not," said Silas. "She must be returned."

"Aye!" came the consensus, and the crowd, as one, began to advance.

Sarah stood rooted, lips defiant, clutching the bewildered child.

Then someone pointed, open-mouthed, and fell on all fours. "The girl's doll – it weeps!"

A gasp rose.

A wet trail dripped from the straw doll's button eye.

"'Tis a sign from the Lord himself!"

"Aye, He wills it not."

"Dare we defy Him?"

"Let her keep the girl!"

Abby glanced at Jacob, as a drop of rain splashed her nose.

Chapter Forty-One

Home

No execution took place that afternoon. The sweet taste for it was gone, replaced by something more bitter and shameful.

Silas Grimston, determined to save face, offered the inquisitors one last chance to leave the village. "I'll seek you out on the morrow," he told them. "And if I find you, our ropes shall feast on your throats."

When nobody cheered, he turned his bile on Obadiah Larke, who pleaded and grovelled to no avail.

The last Abby and Jacob saw of the parson, he was being dragged, bound in rope, to his own lock-up.

"You returned to Brampton?" Abby asked Sarah Watson, once they were safely out of sight.

"They meant to hang you. I couldn't have that on my conscience."

"What will you do now?"

Sarah smiled down at Lency and squeezed her shoulders. The child pulled her doll to her chest, staring at the inquisitors. Jacob sat on his haunches so their faces were level, about to speak. The little girl stuck out her tongue and scurried behind her mother's back.

Jacob grinned sheepishly. "I have never understood children."

"Our home in Wychwood is all but ash, and I'm done with hiding," Sarah told Abby. "Yet I shall not return to Brampton. Its folk are vicious and foolish. Perhaps we'll move to Huntingdon, or leave the county altogether. We have a few coins to our name."

Jacob twitched at the mention.

"And Lency's mother?" Abby asked.

Sarah's lips pursed. "I told you, I…"

"Aye, Sarah, I know."

"They were right. Dotty Nettlewood was but sixteen when the parson paid her off. Unfit to raise a child, she fled the village gossip and Larke's evil. 'Tis why I took her, and we left for Wychwood all those years ago - and why we revived the Drummer."

"You weren't hounded from the village?"

Sarah snorted. "There's the gossip I spoke of - most of it untrue." Then her face softened. "I must return to my husband, we have plans to make. But I would thank you first. Your words and kindness inspired me. I'd ne'er have set foot in Brampton without you."

The women embraced. "We're fortunate you did. You saved our lives," Abby said. "The debt is all ours."

The sun was setting as they returned to the Pepyses'. Their employer was waiting, having returned from London, seated for supper with his parents and sister.

"Jacob! Abigail!" Samuel cried, leaping from his chair. "Where have you been? I have endured the most arduous of days! My coach lost a wheel and there was a hole in its roof that soaked my new hat."

Jacob looked to Abby, about to retort, when she gave the smallest shake of her head.

"May we sit?" she asked. "We, too, have had a trying day."

"Let me fetch you some supper," said Margaret, rising. "Venison pasty with turnip."

"Indeed, indeed," Samuel blustered, pulling out chairs for his inquisitors. "What have you discovered? Have you found my gold?"

Everyone leaned forward.

Mr Pepys's gold had been the least of the inquisitors' worries, though they did not voice it. Frankly, in the battle to save their necks it had been all but forgotten.

Yet Abby's reply left Jacob slack-jawed.

"I have an inkling," she said, "that I know where 'tis hidden."

The drawing of breaths seemed to suck the air from the room.

"Then return it at once, Abigail!" Samuel snapped. "This instant, I tell you!"

Abby lowered her head, eyes fixed on her esteemed employer. "You've said before that you trust me?"

Pepys wobbled his jowls. "Indeed, yet I see no reason…"

"Then I ask that you trust me again, sir. We have disappointed you before, and I would hate to do so again with so much at stake. As I said, 'tis merely a suspicion. Jacob and I shall act upon it ere we are too late, I assure you. I wouldn't wish," she glanced at Paulina, who had returned to her turnip, "to forewarn the miscreant. We must do so at the dead of night."

"Tonight?" Samuel asked, leaning into the table.

She nodded. "I swear it, sir."

At length he was placated, and the inquisitors dined as never before. Jacob called for a second serving and was obliged to loosen his breeches. However, when he reached to top up his goblet, Abby slipped a hand over it.

"We shall need our wits about us," she said quietly.

"Tell me," he replied. "What…?"

"Not now," she cut him off. Their employer had, for the moment at least, forgotten all about his stolen coin, and she wished to keep it that way.

Their tales were still being told long after John, Margaret and Paulina had retired to their beds. Abby and Jacob took turns recalling their nights in Wychwood, their dealings with the Watsons, and their flight through the nunnery's secret tunnels.

"There are tunnels 'neath the estate itself? Which run all about Brampton?" Samuel asked, incredulous.

Jacob puffed out his chest. "Indeed, sir. A rat-faced fellow named Croot dwells in them."

Samuel filled his goblet to the brim. "Croot, you say?"

"Amos Croot," Abby said, sipping her small beer. "The same rat-faced fellow who helped us escape the Grimstons' mob when they were out for our blood."

Jacob harrumphed, and she sat back, sighing contentedly to herself.

There were nights when her family had settled before a hearty fire, as they were now, sharing stories and making merry. Her father, Ambrose, could be cheery once a long day's printing commissions were finished, when he would settle in his favoured chair, ale in hand. He would talk on any subject, from royalty to revolution, and she would stretch across his lap as he stroked her hair.

He had died in The Clink jail nearly two years ago. *Two years*, she mused. *How lives change.*

In some ways - though not before leaving his service, naturally - Mr Pepys now felt like a father figure. He was fond of her; she could see it sometimes in the way he looked at her, unable to conceal a pout of pride. He had cared for her, educated and housed her, put food in her belly, and set her on this path that had granted her worth.

And yet… he was no Ambrose Harcourt.

Jacob was glad that Mr Pepys was not his father. Sir Miles Standish, the late naval surveyor - Pepys's equal in rank and friend besides - had been strict, yet fair. How else would Jacob have tackled those fiendish sums, had Sir Miles not soundly thrashed him?

Then again… it occurred to him, he had routinely failed to solve the calculations.

Pepys had never thrashed him - shouted perhaps, or fallen moodily silent - but had treated him with fairness and dignity. Jacob wondered where he might be without the man.

Indeed, he was no Miles Standish.

And so the night drew in, with Samuel growing drunk.

It would help him sleep, Abby reasoned, having refilled his goblet more than once. The last thing she and Jacob needed was his fussing when their time came to act.

And act they would, very soon.

Chapter Forty-Two

The Summerhouse

When Samuel Pepys awoke the next morning, he was aware of his swollen, dry tongue and throbbing head. Then, like a bolt from the heavens, it struck him: his gold!

He was up and out of his bed in a trice.

The sun had long since risen, and he cursed his slovenliness as he descended the stairs two at a time, all but collapsing in a heap at the bottom.

"Jacob! Abigail!" he cried, peering first into the kitchen - where his mother was kneading dough - and then into the hall, to find his father dozing in a chair.

"Jacob! Abigail!"

John Pepys jerked awake. "Cease your shouting, lad," he muttered, wiping drool from his chin. "You'll wake the dead."

"Mr Pepys!" came the call from outside. "Out here! In the summerhouse!"

"Dress yourself ere you step outside, Sam," John said.

But his son was already gone.

As through much of the winter, the sun that morning was too weak to melt the frost, which crunched beneath his bare feet as he ran. He felt no chill in his soles.

"Have you found it?" he demanded breathlessly.

His inquisitors were standing outside the summer-house, a blackened, battered handcart beside them. It was not Pepys's, though he felt sure he had seen it before. Jacob nudged Abby, who kept a straight face, pride fit to burst.

Pepys halted, wheezing, clutching his linen nightshirt about him. "Tell me, I beseech you! Spare me this agony."

Jacob reached out and opened the summerhouse door.

There lay five bulging canvas sacks, plastered in mud and brimming with gold.

Pepys flung himself inside, crying out with glee, scooping up broad pieces as though he scarcely believed them real. As he held them to his face, brown eyes bog-gling, a shaft of sunlight pierced the summerhouse and hit the hoard. For a brief moment, his waxy skin seemed to glow, as if he were an angel.

He most surely was not.

"Where did you find it?" he asked in disbelief. "Which scoundrel stole it?"

"Would you have us show you, sir?" Abby asked.

Recalling the Demon

Pepys dressed in such haste that his buttons were in all the wrong holes, his shirt askew, and his stockings rumpled in his shoes. He did not care.

Jacob led them out into the meadow at the rear of the house, past Rebecca Thacker's cottage, toward the church.

Veering west, they came upon The Bull, where they drew to a halt.

"This is no time for ale, Mr Standish," Pepys snapped. "I wish to set eyes upon the men who caused me such anguish."

The inn stood broken in the morning mist, its damaged roof stark against the sky. No candles burned in the windows, and no sound came from within.

Abby knocked on the door.

"They've gone," she affirmed, then headed for the rear of the inn. "Come."

At the outbuildings, she glanced down the road toward the lock-up opposite the church. She pictured Parson Larke in there, praying on the cold stone floor, and found no mercy in her heart.

When they found the little wooden cross scratched with the name 'RUSTY', she stopped. The soil in the grave looked freshly dug.

"Here," she said, "is where your coin lay concealed."

"In a mutt's grave?" Pepys spluttered.

"Where better?" Abby replied. "None would dream of looking there. We came across Hatty digging it - she told us she was planting flowers."

"Yet there were no flowers," Jacob added.

"Aye, since 'tis winter. So glad were we to see her, we failed to pay heed."

Jacob pushed a toe into the loose soil. "Your hoard was first hidden in the hermit house in Wychwood. They revived the Drummer to frighten folk from those parts. Later they panicked, fearful we were closing in, and moved it. Since they were set to leave Brampton, they buried it nearby."

Pepys stamped a foot in frustration. "And who, pray, is *they*?"

Jacob nodded to Abby.

She licked her lips. "'Twas the innkeeper and his wife, Barty and Hatty Nettlewood, sir. In league with the physician and stablemaid. Yet it seems they fell out, since Bramwell and Wilkins now lie dead."

"Barty and Hatty Nettlewood?" Pepys exclaimed, pressing palms to his temples. "But why, in God's name?"

Jacob shrugged. "They overheard talk of buried treasure, sir. Untold riches. An end to drudgery. Who would not?"

Pepys squared up to him. "I would not, Mr Standish! The very thought appals me."

The inquisitors stared at the ground.

As Pepys's anger boiled, memories flickered of the silver plate, pouches of coin and barrels of oysters pressed upon him in return for valuable naval contracts. He cast them aside as irrelevant.

His heart pounded in his chest, and he composed himself. "How did you know 'twas the Nettlewoods? What is your proof?"

Abby turned to Jacob. "Remember the Demon of Spreyton?"

He frowned.

"The servant, Francis Fey, who saw the ghost of his master's father," she pressed.

He slapped a fist into his palm. "That scoundrel! Concocting spirits to fleece the gullible."

She nodded. "Aye, and just as Francis Fey manufactured a ghost for profit, so too did the Nettlewoods." She paused. "Remember what Hatty Nettlewood told us of the Drummer? She said: 'I heard it first'. 'Twas she who started the whispers, to keep folk from Wychwood where the hoard lay hidden."

Jacob scratched his chin. "Then 'twas the Nettlewoods we heard and saw, playing the ghost?"

"Indeed. The rising cloaked figure in the wood was Barty lifting his wife with the aid of a pulley."

Pepys tutted. "This is all but hearsay."

"Aye, sir, but once I realised late in our inquiry that 'twas Hatty Nettlewood herself who had revived the Drummer, all fell into place."

Archibald Bramwell's mother had told him of the Pepys gold, she said, after Margaret revealed it in a fever. As an esteemed physician, mindful of his reputation, Bramwell wrestled with the desire to act, and later confided in his lover, Alice Wilkins. Drunk, they spoke carelessly at The Bull, where the Nettlewoods overheard the pair quarrelling over the gold one night.

"They must have made a pact between them," Abby said, "but needed your house empty to dig up the five sacks from the herb garden. Bramwell arranged your parents' visit, sir, to test their eyes, at ten of the clock on January the fourth - the night of the theft.

Pepys's eyes widened. "My own family, used as pawns?"

"Indeed, sir. And where was Paulina that same night? At The Bull with Harry Packer, where Hatty was 'free with her pitchers', Paulina told us. Thus Hatty and Bramwell kept your family away, while Barty and Alice stole the gold. They took his handcart, suspecting the haul would be too heavy to carry - as it proved."

Pepys began to pace. "Yet they fell out, you say."

"At first, there was safety in numbers. Once the hoard's size was revealed, each coveted the other's share. When we arrived in Brampton - feted inquisitors, having cleared Paulina of witchery - panic set in, and disagreement festered till it grew fatal.

"Bramwell's discarded cloak smelled of smoke, and I believe he set The Bull aflame, hoping to murder the Nettlewoods before they could commit the same. He'd turned to drink, his judgment unsound and his tongue loose. Through fear and greed, Barty strangled him in his study - his arms were scratched from the struggle." She turned to Jacob. "After Barty heard us tell Harry Packer of finding Bramwell's body, did you notice he disappeared? 'Twas Hatty who served our drink."

Jacob gripped her arm. "He left to murder poor Alice Wilkins, ere she could tell?"

She tilted her head. "We found her cold body the next day."

Pepys spotted crumpled paper discarded beside Rusty's grave. When he stooped to retrieve it, a glance passed between the inquisitors.

Unfolding it, Pepys read aloud: "'We know what you did'." He stiffened. "'We know what you did'?"

"We left it, sir," Jacob said. "For the Nettlewoods. A small… jest."

Abby cringed at the word - Pepys was incapable of finding his stolen coin amusing. "What Jacob means is," she said, "we wished them to know we were onto them."

Pepys's nostrils flared. "When did they leave Brampton?"

Abby spoke before Jacob could. "I saw Barty packing yesterday. 'Tis why I knew we had to find your gold last night, or 'twould be gone forever. Their carts, brimming with crates and sacks, were still here when we arrived in the early hours."

"And you allowed them to escape?" Pepys bellowed.

A young lad was repairing beechwood fencing up the lane, and Pepys called to him. "You! Boy! Come here this instant!"

The lad arrived, wringing his hands. "Sir?"

"Did the Nettlewoods pass by you with horse and cart this morning?"

"Aye, sir, they did. Not long after dawn. She was raging at him, and he looked most distressed - as if he'd seen a ghost, sir."

Chapter Forty-Four

A Hasty Pledge

Mr Pepys stomped ahead, fretting that his precious coin now lay unguarded in the summerhouse.

Jacob slowed, motioning for Abby to do the same. "Did we allow the Nettlewoods to escape?"

"How could we have taken both them and the gold?"

He ran a thumb across his lips, lost in thought. "They seemed such decent folk. Hard-working, amenable. Yet…"

"Money changes people, Jacob. The poor covet it, the rich hoard it. We thought we knew the Nettlewoods." She walked on. "We did not."

When he caught up, she stopped and pressed her brooch into his hand. It felt in that moment like a vulgar trinket. "You must have it," she said.

He gave a curt laugh and pushed it away. "It does not suit me."

"Then if you will not have it," she tossed it into Rebecca Thacker's garden, "neither shall I."

He grasped her arm. "I was consumed by jealousy, Abby. I…"

She took his hand. "And I was too easily swayed by fanciful dreams of fame upon the King's stage. We are best where we are - as inquisitors. It befits us."

As they neared the Pepyses' cottage, she said softly, "I'll never forget your words at the gallows, Jacob."

"I meant them, each and every one."

"I know," she said, slipping into the garden.

After dinner, the Pepyses, Abby and Jacob gathered around the table in the hall. Samuel had sent for a Navy Board coach to take them home, accompanied by armed men to guard his hoard.

The five sacks lay hidden under the table, while a Brampton constable stood watch at the door. Some colour had returned to John Pepys's cheeks in his joy - and relief - at the return of the gold.

The mood was jubilant, and the Pepyses' finest wine had been opened.

As Margaret arrived with a trencher of oysters, men's voices arguing came from outside.

"Harry!" Paulina cried, rushing to the door.

Pepys glowered. "I would give all my gold to see that dreadful man removed from my sister's life," he told Abby seated next to him.

"All of it?" she asked sweetly.

Chapter Forty-Five

By Royal Appointment

Harry Packer, having lost his mind, threatened to shoot Samuel Pepys in the back before being knocked unconscious. "As I did this man whose coat I stole!" he raged, before the fall of the constable's club. It explained the darned holes in the fabric.

The two pages Abby had torn from the parish record lay side by side on the table - all the proof she had needed to accuse Packer of being the Grimstons' cousin. He had not taken it well.

Upstairs, Margaret and John consoled a weeping Paulina.

"'Twas Jacob who alerted me to it." Abby told the still trembling Pepys, hands clutching his wine.

"Aye, sir," Jacob added brightly. "I spied four tankards at the Grimston house…"

"Then later, when the parson chased away the straw-haired man digging by his elder, I assumed it was Packer, yet…"

"I pointed out he is not the only one with such hair…"

"You said, 'What of the Grimstons?'" Abby grinned. "And it made me wonder: what if they're related? Packer turned up in Brampton shortly after the Grimston family had been shamed, and latched onto Paulina. Was it love he sought - or revenge?"

"When the brothers waylaid us outside The Bull one night, Elias let slip he knew Harry, and Silas was forced to cover his tracks."

Abby slid one of the papers before Samuel. "I found this record of William Packer's marriage to Bess Grimston, dated January 1637." Then the other. "It led me to this, from December the same year: the birth of their son, Henry. Our Harry Packer."

Jacob nudged Samuel, spilling some of the wine. "Bess Grimston was Goddie's sister, sir, according to the record - making Harry his nephew and Silas Grimston's cousin."

"Quite," Samuel said, eyeing the seeping red on his new white shirt.

"His reaction when I accused him was proof enough," Abby concluded, then delicately cleared her throat. "There was the small matter of a reward, for removing Mr Packer from your sister's life. I do recall you saying you would give 'all your gold'?"

His horrified expression - as if he had woken beside Paulina - would stay with her.

He blustered excuses, waved aside his own contradictions, chuckled unconvincingly, then dug a hand into one of the sacks. Pulling out a handful of broad pieces, he let several spill before emerging with half a dozen.

These, he handed to Abby with his gratitude.

It was six more gold coins than she had ever owned.

Keen to move on – even that loss had him mopping his brow, deathly pale – he tapped the back of Jacob's hand.

"Our next inquiry, sir?" the inquisitor asked eagerly.

"You know me too well." Pepys chuckled. "You are aware of the Crown Jewels?"

Abby and Jacob shot each other a look.

"Whilst in London, I met with His Majesty. He did confide in me word of a most treacherous and audacious plot – to steal the King's treasures from the Tower itself. The city's foremost stronghold." His solemn gaze shifted from Jacob to Abby. "He commands that my inquisitors foil it."

Though the prospect of the King's patronage – following their torrid time at his court – pleased neither greatly, it was a sure sign of their rising station.

Jacob stared at Pepys in disbelief. "King Charles himself commissions us?"

Pepys coughed politely. "Commands, Jacob. Word of your success has spread. This is indeed a great honour."

"What if we fail?" Abby asked, feeling for her agate brooch and remembering its fate.

Pepys peered down his nose at her. "But you will not. Of that I am assured."

"I accept His Majesty's command gladly, sir," said Jacob. "There is just one thing…?"

"What is it, Jacob?"

"Promise me we shall never return to Brampton."

If you enjoyed this book, please consider leaving a rating or review – they are greatly appreciated and genuinely help.

Next up: trapped in the indomitable Tower, Abby and Jacob meet their most dangerous adversary yet, in The Samuel Pepys Mysteries Book 8: The Crown Jewels Murders.
Amazon link: mybook.to/pepys-series

- "This series just gets better with every book" – *Rambling Mads*

- "A gripping and fascinating read" – *Curling Up with a Coffee and a Kindle*

- "The Samuel Pepys Mystery series never disappoints. Every book is well-researched and superbly written" – *Cozy Crime Reads*

Read All Nine!

mybook.to/pepys-series

Ellis Blackwood

Ellis Blackwood fell in love with the writings of Samuel Pepys and the 17th-century England he so colourfully portrays via the great man's published diaries. The Samuel Pepys Mysteries are the result of that literary love affair.

Ellis lives on the coast of Cornwall with his wife, two daughters and dog, Spike. A former journalist, he wrote features for many of the UK's most popular national newspapers and magazines. During the COVID lockdown, he gained an MA in Comedy Writing.

Visit my website ellisblackwood.com for all release updates, and to subscribe to my monthly newsletter – including the FREE Pepys Mysteries introductory novella, Mr Pepys's Stolen Diaries.

Find me on Facebook @ellisblackwoodauthor

And on Instagram @ellisblackwood_author

Scan the QR code for all my links.

Acknowledgements

I could not have published The Samuel Pepys Mysteries without the sterling work of Tim Brown, whose covers are a joy to behold, and whose editorial guidance has been a godsend. Equally, my wife, Sinead, has worked tirelessly and generously in the background to allow me the time and space to research, write, and drink far too much tea.

If you'd like to learn more about Samuel Pepys and 17th century England, I recommend starting here:

- *The Illustrated Pepys* edited by Robert Latham, Penguin Books (1979)

- *London and the 17th Century* by Margarette Lincoln, Yale University Press (2021)

- *Samuel Pepys: The Unequalled Self* by Claire

Tomalin, Penguin Books (2003)

- *The Time Traveller's Guide to Restoration Britain* by Ian Mortimer, The Bodley Head (2017)

In my monthly newsletters, I deep-dive into the fascinating historical background to each novel, from the Princes in the Tower to the ingredients of posset. Visit ellisblackwood.comto sign up.